Who Would You Kill
to Save the World?

SERIES EDITORS

Marco Abel and Roland Végső

PROV
OCAT
IONS

Something in the world forces us to think.
—Gilles Deleuze

The world provokes thought. Thinking is nothing but the human response to this provocation. Thus, the very nature of thought is to be the product of a provocation. This is why a genuine act of provocation cannot be the empty rhetorical gesture of the contrarian. It must be an experimental response to the historical necessity to act. Unlike the contrarian, we refuse to reduce provocation to a passive noun or a state of being. We believe that real moments of provocation are constituted by a series of actions that are best defined by verbs or even infinitives—verbs in a modality of potentiality, of the promise of action. To provoke is to intervene in the present by invoking an as yet undecided future radically different from what is declared to be possible in the present and, in so doing, to arouse the desire for bringing about change. By publishing short books from multiple disciplinary perspectives that are closer to the genres of the manifesto, the polemical essay, the intervention, and the pamphlet than to traditional scholarly monographs, "Provocations" hopes to serve as a forum for the kind of theoretical experimentation that we consider to be the very essence of thought.

www.provocationsbooks.com

Who Would You Kill to Save the World?

CLAIRE COLEBROOK

UNIVERSITY OF NEBRASKA PRESS · LINCOLN

The University of Nebraska Press is part
of a land-grant institution with campuses
and programs on the past, present, and
future homelands of the Pawnee, Ponca,
Otoe-Missouria, Omaha, Dakota, Lakota,
Kaw, Cheyenne, and Arapaho Peoples,
as well as those of the relocated Ho-
Chunk, Sac and Fox, and Iowa Peoples.

Library of Congress
Cataloging-in-Publication Data
Names: Colebrook, Claire, author.
Title: Who would you kill to save
the world? / Claire Colebrook.
Description: Lincoln: University of Nebraska
Press, [2023] | Series: Provocations |
Includes bibliographical references.
Identifiers: LCCN 2022055950
ISBN 9781496234988 (paperback)
ISBN 9781496237156 (epub)
ISBN 9781496237163 (pdf)
Subjects: LCSH: Apocalyptic films—History
and criticism. | Motion pictures—United
States—History—21st century. | BISAC: SOCIAL
SCIENCE / Media Studies | FICTION / Science
Fiction / Apocalyptic & Post-Apocalyptic
Classification: LCC PN1995.9.A64 C65 2023 |
DDC 791.43/615—dc23/eng/20230213
LC record available at https://
lccn.loc.gov/2022055950

Set in Sorts Mill Goudy by Mikala R. Kolander.
Designed by N. Putens.

CONTENTS

ACKNOWLEDGMENTS

This book began as a talk delivered at the University of Nebraska in 2019. Since delivering that talk (which was part of the Humanities on the Edge series), I have benefited greatly from the ongoing editorial advice of Marco Abel and Roland Végső. I am also indebted to my Penn State colleagues, Carla Mulford and Marcy North; our odd writing group has helped me immensely.

Prior to forming the idea of this book, I was dragged to film after film by Lee Spinks, whose knowledge of cinema has been an ongoing inspiration. Richard Willis, another cinephile, helped me think about art and philosophy beyond its bookish forms.

This book is dedicated to Sue Loukomitis.

PROVOCATIONS

After all, it's not the end of the world.

Well, that's just it. It *is* the end of the world. Every day another collapse, another catastrophe, another emergency, another tipping point, and another feeble attempt to avert the end.

No, it's not. It's not the end of the world. It's the end of capitalism, the end of humanism, the end of global finance, the end of planet-gouging resource extraction, the end of neoliberalism, the end of white supremacy, the end of increasingly intensified surveillance technologies, the end of cis-hetero-normativity, the end of settler colonialism, the end of mononaturalism, and the end of patriarchy.

What's left?

What's left is the world. We need to save the world.

But there's so much that needs to be destroyed to give the world a chance: global finance, liberal humanism, patriarchy, cis-hetero-normativity, settler colonialism . . . How can we ever clear away all that's needed to save the world?

Really, it's simple. What you think of as the world, and what you think of as desperately worthy of being saved, has already required so much destruction and annihilation. . . . *So much attempted world-ending* in order to "save the world." What you think of as the end of the world is the end of "too big to fail" logic. You need to save the world, not capitalism.

What's left?

What's left is everything we are willing to live and die for.

PREFACE

This book is ostensibly about cinema and the end of the world. More specifically, it is about how certain forms of cinema reduce the end of the world to a privatized and commodified spectacle. These forms of cinema have a prehistory, both in modern philosophy and the novel. To say that the end of the world is a cinematic event is not just to notice the extent to which twenty-first-century culture endlessly rehearses the end of the world; it is also to note that what counts as *the world* has been the outcome of centuries of cinematic thinking. The world that ends in contemporary cinema is a world of anonymous and meaningless destruction; we in the cinema witness and enjoy global catastrophe. That same world is then saved by one of us, one of the privileged few capable of surveying and mastering the whole. Twenty-first-century cinema makes explicit what was silently assumed in so much modern literature and philosophy: however diverse and complex the globe may be, there is a point of view from which the world might be surveyed, saved, and rendered worthy. That point of view is the private individual subject, for whom the spectacle of loss and injustice is the occasion both to affirm the right to life of the future and to look back on the past as nothing more than a journey toward redemption.

What happens when we go to the cinema—at least in its

classic (prestreaming, pre-ultra-privatized) mode? As a group, we watch a narrative unfold within a tolerable duration; we are safe but exposed to all sorts of horrors and sadnesses. We occupy a static position but can experience a flow of time that flashes back and forth; and whatever chaos and loss we may witness, we can walk away. At times, the produced "we" of cinema viewing is apparent: we all scream, cry, laugh, or wince in common. Those collective affects have a prehistory, a set of attachments and desires that give narrative coherence to cinematic time. It is through the experiences of cinema that we become who we are, attached to certain ways of living, oriented to certain forms of time and space, and oriented to certain possible futures. This becomes especially apparent in save-the-world cinema. Various threats to the world—from zombies and pandemics to climate catastrophe and alien invasion—intensify and justify who we are. Nothing galvanizes one's sense of a right to life quite like the possibility of annihilation.

One of the claims of this book is that most Hollywood cinema is save-the-world cinema. In addition to the flourishing genre of postapocalyptic narratives, there are the conclusions that reinforce the family, the couple, or the state. *Everything Everywhere All at Once*, directed by Daniel Kwan and Daniel Scheinert in 2022, flirts with nihilism—where multiple worlds would render any value in *this* world utterly relative—but concludes by reaffirming the family. Even if all we value is relative only to us, tied to the contingent attachments that compose our world, it is the kindness of the family that provides the film with its joyous conclusion. For all its metaphysical sophistication in adopting multiple time lines and the possibility of multiple universes, *Everything Everywhere All at Once* is typical of twenty-first-century Hollywood cinema in posing and then silencing the question of saving the world. Early in the film the central character learns that she must destroy her own daughter in order to avoid the overwhelming chaos that her daughter has embraced—a chaos that follows from understanding that one's own values mean nothing once one goes beyond one's own world. Rather than kill her daughter to save the world, the central character focuses on redeeming her relationship to her daughter. The answer to nihilism, relativism, and the cruel contingency of the world turns out to be the family, and especially the maternal bond. All we need is love. Hollywood cinema's reiteration of individual and familial triumph extends and intensifies the form and affective attachments of the modern novel. Why cinema becomes so important at the end of the world is its capacity to contract global catastrophe into the point of view and narrative of the individual. Hollywood, and especially postapocalyptic cinema, intensifies the triumphal heroism of novelistic individualism and ties the individual's and family's redemption to an unquestioned task of saving the world. Perhaps all forms of art rely on saving the world or preserving something that is assumed to be worthy, but what makes twenty-first-century cinema so remarkable is its odd coupling of saving *the world* with the point of view of the private and privatized individual.

By posing the end of *the* world, postapocalyptic cinema renders explicit our attachment to quite specific modes of existence. If a James Bond film saves the world by fighting off foreign espionage, and an alien-invasion epic saves the world by destroying a spaceship, or a global-pandemic blockbuster vanquishes a zombifying virus, then all these possible ends produce a world that appears unquestionably worth saving. What would happen if one were to adopt the point of view of the Russian, Korean, or (depending on the geopolitical situation) variously otherwise-foreign agents in a Bond film *or* if one were to adopt the point of view of the alien—someone whose world is *not* ours?

The twenty-first century no longer needs to imagine alien invasion, malevolent superpowers, or zombifying viruses that will end the world. Daily missives from the Intergovernmental Panel on Climate Change (the IPCC), global pandemics, evidence of the sixth mass extinction, and the declaration that the earth has now shifted to a new geological era of the Anthropocene pose the imminent possibility of the end, but the end of what? This is where explicitly postapocalyptic cinema intersects with art and politics: the end of the world is not the end of the planet; it is the end of a specific mode of existence. What we value and who we are become readable through the narratives we create and consume. Just who we are and what is worth saving starts to become a more explicit problem. To what extent is the world that we are seeking to save a world that is essentially careening toward an end? Every romance novel that ends with a marriage affirms the institution of the family; every postapocalyptic film that threatens our world with an end intensifies our attachment to who we are and our desire to survive. Not all uses of point of view are parochial. There is a long literary and cinematic tradition of using point of view to challenge attachments that compose our world. If the early novel begins by affirming the enterprising individual who finds marriage and fortune, the subsequent history of the novel plays with point of view, time, and attachments. Every television series that charts the path of a serial killer (*Dexter*), a mafia boss (*The Sopranos*), or a drug dealer (*Breaking Bad*) plays with the limits of our normative affects. Such narratives expose the ways in which sympathies and affects are formed simply by following the trajectory of a life. By tracking the decisions, desires, and affects of a character, narratives transform (or reinforce) sympathies and attachments. Because we are feeling with an other, there is a degree of attachment that allows the narrative to continue as a desire simply to survive. If the character dies, the narrative ends; and if the world ends, the narrative dies. Most Hollywood films allow loss and disaster to be steps in the stages of a morality tale. Stephen Spielberg's

Saving Private Ryan (1998) opens with the devastating carnage of war, only to proceed with a narrative that affirms the beauty and justice of human fidelity. From mass death to individual actions of kindness, it is the zooming in of Hollywood cinema that enables global disaster to become a private and personal affair. Disaster, no matter how global, becomes background collateral damage if *we* survive; who we are is the effect of these spectacles and dramas of surviving. The claim of this book is that this attachment to and desire for survival becomes clear in postapocalyptic cinema but goes well beyond cinema. Who we are is the effect of attachments and point of view.

When there is talk about the end of the world as we know it—and such talk has intensified in the twenty-first century—it becomes necessary and urgent to ask who this "we" is and how this world is known. Sometimes these questions concern parochial attachments. In 2016 Donald Trump's presidential campaign of Make America Great Again could only make sense if there were some attachment to America's past, some sense of a past that was more properly *ours*. Every government tax cut, every higher education initiative, every green policy, every purchase an individual makes, and every dollar we donate (or don't) relies on, and sustains, an attachment to a certain world. For some—the affluent Westerners who are depicted as the world-saving and savable characters in postapocalyptic cinema—maintaining their world requires an ongoing toll on other worlds. Not all cinema and literature is world saving in this uncritical sense. Some forms of literature and cinema foreground the problem of cinema and its prehistory, and do so by creating lines of time and sympathy that pose the question of just whose world is being saved and whose lives become so much collateral damage for the sake of reaffirming who we are.

Jordan Peele's *Nope* (2022) depicts the end of several worlds. The most apparent world-ending narrative thread of the film concerns an alien spaceship that consumes humans. The narrative follows a brother and sister who seek to capture (on film) and annihilate the human-devouring aliens. The only way to avoid being consumed by what appears to be a ship that is also an organism is to avoid looking or directing one's eyes toward the ship as it sucks up humans for sustenance. It is as though *looking* is the first step to losing one's self. The ship's path across the landscape shuts off all forms of energy, reducing the humans in its range to powerless animals who can then be readily snatched from their worlds and consumed. Alongside this alien-invasion narrative is a metacinematic thread regarding cinema and erasure; the central characters are descendants of the first human to appear on film—a Black man riding a horse. His grandchildren now manage a farm that provides horses to Hollywood and—after falling on hard times—to a themed ranch run by a former child TV star. What ties these two threads together is the problem of visibility and survival. Humans can easily become prey in a war of visual technologies; the alien predators disable human media (such as security cameras and lighting) and lure human victims by capturing their attention. Hollywood's visual capture, erasure, and animalization of Black bodies enables the alien-invasion thread of the film to be read as an allegory. Just as aliens will disable, consume, and capture humans, so Hollywood (and America in general) erased the histories and lives of those it put on display, always relying on capturing and diverting attention away from its violence.

The allegorical dimension of *Nope* is accompanied by a powerful existential dimension. The film opens with a picture of a chimpanzee in a living room that turns out to be the TV set of a sitcom, where the star chimpanzee went rogue and massacred the cast (all except the remaining child star who now runs the ranch theme park that becomes the locale for vanquishing, as well as filming or capturing, the aliens). In all three narrative strands, it is the animalized who fight back. In all three strands, a world—that of the aliens, Hollywood and thereby America, and humanity—relies on capturing and consuming others. In the case of Gordy the chimpanzee, the human myth of the comic animal there for our enjoyment and spectacle occludes the violence of assuming the other is there for *our pleasure*. Peele's *Nope* is manifestly yet one more tale about killing *them* to save *us*, with the film charting the triumph of two horse trainers over the human-eating ship. The allegorical strand frames this endeavor within a morality tale about Hollywood and America: the grandchildren of Hollywood's erased Black first man take up cameras and capture images of the human-consuming ship as it meets its end. The existential frame of the film places these two dimensions within the problem of survival in general: who are we such that our lives are worth the destruction and consumption of others? This is a political and racial question, as the world we enjoy is only possible through the animalization, erasure, and capture of those deemed not worthy of being saved, while the *narrative* of that calculation is increasingly cinematic.

Bernard Stiegler referred to the earliest human paintings as forms of "arche-cinema"; to view a cave painting was to experience the desire and imagination of another human whose experiences were stored and retained into a future. Every subsequent cave painting adds to and transforms the ways in which humans imagine themselves and their world. This book is concerned with a quite specific mutation of that early form of memory storage and desire formation. What happens when such imaginings become industrialized and when a single industry (such as Hollywood cinema) produces a genre that is at once consumed and disseminated globally while also using the form of a highly privatized individual point of view? What has come to be known as postapocalyptic cinema frequently presents the end of the world, but it does so from the point of view of the private individual. Although cinema makes this contraction and privatization of the end of the world particularly apparent, there is a prehistory of this privatization of collectivity in other cultural forms, such as the novel. From collective experiences of stored memories, modernity has increasingly privatized and industrialized the forms of the imagination, producing an assumed "we" that is composed from isolated individuals. What is explicit in cinema of the twenty-first century—the affirmation of a single world that is worth saving despite its past and present injustices—has a formal structure and narrative that extends well beyond cinema. Policy and political discourse assume the same "we" of private individuals and the same narrative structure of a world that is progressively just and rational and therefore the only world worth saving. Just as cinema in its postapocalyptic and mass-produced form produces narratives almost solely from the point of view of isolated and heroic individuals, allowing global destruction to be reduced to a familial drama of redemption, it is also generally assumed that the only world worth saving is the world of late capitalist and privatized consumption.

The form of a certain type of cinema structures twenty-first-century culture more generally: catastrophes become the occasion for salvation, and the spectacle of loss becomes the occasion for human triumphalism. What was typical of the modern novel—a narrative of individual triumph over adversity—has transformed in twenty-first-century cinema to become an individual triumphing over planetary catastrophe. The end of the world has been personalized and privatized. The spectacle and speculation on all the possible threats to humanity becomes a commodity one might enjoy, and becomes the occasion to reiterate the point of view of liberal individualism. The world becomes a scene to be surveyed, reaffirming the rights and reasons of the managerial subject of capitalism.

**Who Would You Kill
to Save the World?**

1

It's Not the End of the World

It might seem to be common sense to suppose that one would want to do everything in one's power to avoid the end of the world. The everyday phrase of consolation—"it's not the end of the world"—would seem to suggest that we can place all other losses into perspective insofar as they fall short of the end of the world. This everyday weak stoicism has come under recent and intense pressure; the day-to-day worries that assault us do appear to be the end of the world. This can range from power outages in snowstorms and heat waves that are now signs of climate change to the ongoing attrition of voting rights, health care, racial justice, and education. It is now possible to think that certain events *are* the end of the world, or at least the beginning of the end. Doing what one can to avert the end of the world is no longer a question posed in moments of rare crisis; "saving the world" is no longer the task of superheroes in blockbuster epics but presents itself as an ongoing drama in everyday life. Global pandemics, flagrant fascism, extreme climate catastrophes, the increased visibility of white supremacist movements, refugee crises and immigrant detention centers, toxic water, and resource scarcity all suggest that the life we live now *is* bordering on the end of the world. The end of the world is upon us; the "us" now faced with the world's end often does so by imagining itself as threatened with becoming *just like them*. From Enlightenment visions of rational cosmopolitanism, where the affluent West depicted itself as moving toward increasing inclusion and unification, the twenty-first century is dominated with visions of the West becoming like the spaces it had set itself to redeem. The unification of global humanity that was once the dream of Enlightenment humanism is now the horror scenario of Anthropocene imaginings; there will be no lifeboats for the rich,[1] now that we are all in the same boat.[2] One of the claims of this book is that this world that now appears to be ending was made possible through centuries of "saving the world." The world that now appears to be threatened has always sought to save itself, either from its non-Western others *or* from its less angelic tendencies.[3] What makes twenty-first-century "end-of-world" culture distinct from centuries of imagined collapse and decay is that saving the world becomes increasingly parochial—saving the world amounts to saving *us*, and the end of the world looks a lot like the affluent West becoming like those others it once sought to save.

Apocalyptic cinema increasingly uses images drawn from the present (such as detention centers and refugee camps) to depict a future in which "we" are now subjected to the conditions long suffered by the colonized, enslaved, indentured, and stateless. Postapocalyptic cinema is often poised between allegory, such that the dystopian future is really an intensification of where we already are, and outright existential dystopia, where we simply imagine ourselves as if we had become *like them*. A film such as *Snowpiercer* (Bong Joon-ho, 2013) might be read allegorically. After a failed geoengineering effort has frozen the planet, a train that has saved a remaining group of humans circles the earth as a self-sufficient ecosystem. The poor are huddled at the back of the train, while the front of the train's elites enjoy hyperconsumption. The poor are also regularly lured into revolution, which serves to cull the surplus population and keep the train going. If *Snowpiercer* is an allegory of capitalism and its built-in capacities to exploit revolution, such scenarios are also future dystopias—a world in which some of *us* are now experiencing the conditions of the stateless. Postapocalyptic dystopias are both allegories of the present—scenes of the injustice directed to the world's poor—*and* horror scenarios about what might happen to *us*, the "we" who can (for now) look upon destitution as something that happens to *them*. This book is about this ongoing drama of us and them, the world and the worldless: the formation of who "we" are through a world that must be saved and the destitution of those whom "we" must save. Saving the world, ostensibly, amounts to saving hyperconsumption, even if holding on to who we are requires the destruction of so many other worlds.

The narrative of a progressive world of affluence—where capitalism expands to include all of humanity in a global market of hyperconsumption—has broken down. Dreams of a fully inclusive and felicitous expansion of Western freedom have transformed into holding on to the last vestige of humanity in an era of systemic collapse. Naomi Klein may have argued that impending planetary destruction "changes everything" by creating an opportunity for global justice, but postapocalyptic cinema has imagined the world otherwise.[4] Climate change becomes the occasion to double down, to insist that because we are threatened, we must survive. In the twenty-first century so many end-of-world dramas have "happy endings" that amount to seeing most of the globe destroyed while a surviving fragment of proper humanity secures a future now redeemed from its less-than-human past. *I Am Legend* (Francis Lawrence, 2007) sees its main character willingly meet his death for the sake of handing on a vaccine that will allow a remaining pocket of Americans (in New Hampshire) to rebuild the world in the wake of a zombie apocalypse. That common narrative structure—of a threatened world that is saved when a small fragment of privileged humanity survives after seeing the rest of the globe fall away—discloses a great deal about coping with the end of the world. In an age of resource depletion and planetary disaster, there is a flourishing genre of popular culture that imagines that the world could end, and yet "we" would survive and emerge as better and truer versions of ourselves. It turns out that even the end of the world is not the end of the world; it is, instead, an occasion for heroism, humanism, and justification of all we happen to have been for the sake of a future that is truly *ours*.

If postapocalyptic cinema and its heroic narratives of joyous recovery in the wake of global destruction are anything to go by, it is possible to imagine climate catastrophes, biopolitical totalitarianism, and global pandemics as occasions of triumph and self-revelation. Not only is the end of the world *not* the end of the world; it is frequently a postapocalyptic exercise in creating the future as ours alone. *The Day after Tomorrow* (Roland Emmerich, 2004) sees Manhattan suffer from the sudden catastrophe of a new ice age, and yet this event of seemingly planetary and geological scale is followed by the happy ending of the rescue of the central characters and an escape to an international space station. *Into the Storm* (Steven Quale, 2014) sees a family reunited in the wake of ravaging tornadoes. The film concludes with the moral message of humans coming together and finding their better selves in the face of adversity. The catastrophic rains that bring killer alligators into town in *Crawl* (Alexandre Aja, 2019) provide an opportunity for an estranged father to become a hero once again for his champion swimmer daughter. Estranged fathers finding redemption through the weathering of climate catastrophes is a remarkably common motif—evidence of the ways in which even the end of the world can be the occasion for narrative pleasure as long, as it is the globe and planet that suffer and not the threatened pocket of urban affluence, which is portrayed as worthy of sympathy. Save the family; save the world. Postapocalyptic cinema is, at once, an expression of preliminary mourning that gives value to the world we have by imagining its loss and a way of allowing climate catastrophe to fall into the same genre as other disasters that are *not* the end of the world but occasions for affirming the heroism of who we are.

How do we move from consolation, where we might be able to deal with all sorts of harms that are not the end of the world, to a confrontation with the loss of the world? This is neither an abstract nor a new problem, nor one that transcends individuals. Climate change has drawn attention to each individual's footprint and the global costs of daily decisions, and it has done so with an accompanying focus on geographical and political differences among various degrees of consumption and planetary harm. It is as though every day we might live with the haunting sense of the lives lost for the sake of being who "we" are. While there is something lazy in simply attributing the management of climate chaos to individual life choices—as though recycling and buying locally could save the world—every contemporary affluent Western life takes a far greater toll on the planet than those modes of existence that the West colonized and enslaved. How then do "we" think about saving the world if the very "we" that is posing the question is the agent of destruction? And how much sense does it make to talk about agency or even a collective "we" in an age of planetary destruction? A quick glance at contemporary cinema reveals two seemingly incompatible desires: the desire to save the world and a desire for the future to be different from the destruction of the past. This is often played out by presenting disaster and catastrophe as the occasion for a less-than-just humanity to find its proper and ethical self. It is as though end-of-world cinema affirms, at once, the current world's absolute right to exist while also acknowledging its inherent injustice. In part, this is a problem of genre, with climate change disasters taking on the heroic narrative form of blockbuster cinema: the world is threatened, but humans rise above adversity to save the day. More significantly, though, this genre reinforces a humanist chauvinism that precedes cinema in its narrow sense.

What has come to call itself humanity, or the "we" of Western humanism, defines itself against internal and external threats and generates an absolute right to life by way of constantly narrating its possible fall. One might think of Plato's allegory of the cave in the *Republic*, where reason is defined as a turn away from the tendency to be captivated by images, or Immanuel Kant's critical project of modernity, where reason tends toward its own laziness but must struggle to think for itself. More recently, one might think of the anxieties and panic around social media, where our own habits and technologies rob us of our proper being.[5] The idea that we are at war with a threat that is in some ways our own self takes on a peculiar intensity in what is now called the Anthropocene; the present destruction of the planet is deemed to have been caused by an agent who appears to be humanity. Even if a fragment of humanity caused planetary change, we are now united in a common future. The Anthropocene is yet one more heroic disaster epic in which the very threat to who we are allows us to reflect upon, and reform, who we have been. "Humanism" and "humanity" are not simply concepts, nor are they natural kinds. As the formation of the Anthropocene and its associated discourses and industries show only too clearly, a sense of "the human" provides ways of organizing what we take to be true, who we are, what counts as a proper form of existence, and what counts as a possible form. Humanism is an institutional and narrative form that produces a horizon of sense in which we must save who we are, whether that requires annihilating, including, transforming, or appropriating what is *not us*. Humanism is a genre that structures the very possibility of certain disciplines, such as the human sciences and much of philosophy. It is a genre that survives in transformations and reversals, but its constant genre is the ongoing drama of *saving the world*. Well before postapocalyptic cinema and twenty-first-century climate change fictions, the staging of our right to life took on the common form of recognizing the inherent fragility of who we are and our capacity to be less than human. This very threat to who we are generates the imperative of survival, elevating the fragment of "we" that has the privilege to save the world, allowing those who are *not us* to fall away as so much collateral damage. This narrative might be thought of as cinematic insofar as it establishes a central point of view that triumphs over an intruding threat while being able to survey a world of threatened (but not quite so valuable) others. The "we" is formed through narration and viewing.

The standard disaster epic that showed a community vanquish an intrusive foe—sinking cruise liners, killer sharks, burning skyscrapers, alien invasions, viral pandemics—contrasted its small world or community with an external threat. But this same genre has now allowed global disasters to appear as if they were threats to a world, rather than the possibility of the annihilation of all worlds. A film like *The Day after Tomorrow* is ostensibly about a climate catastrophe, and yet the narrative and genre are no different from those of intraworld disasters. There is still a small pocket of affluent humanity that journeys toward a happy ending that allows global destruction to pale into insignificance because the central characters have survived. This imaginative holding on to the world at all costs, this capacity to imagine climate catastrophes as tolerable because they will, after all, not be the end of the world, makes one thing very clear: whatever happens, it's not the end of the world. Somehow humanity will survive, and it will do so because humanity is nothing other than the capacity to emerge heroically from destruction, all the stronger for knowing its unquestionable value.

Within these insistent and compulsively repetitive narratives of necessary world salvation, there is a hint of dissent: the disasters that ravage the world appear more and more to be end points and consequences of the very world that must be saved. In addition to the intrusion of climate change, which is the outcome of the urban affluence that must be saved at all costs, other end-of-world epics see the world threatened with technological overreach, runaway artificial intelligence, corporations becoming tyrannical, and resource depletion leading to political destitution. All these possibilities collide in *Blade Runner 2049* (Denis Villeneuve, 2017), where resource depletion has allowed a corporation to govern the world undemocratically and control life by way of managing the technologies of life—including artificial life. The world that appears to be ending and in urgent need of being saved is the *same* world that bears its destruction within its very means of possibility. It is here that the cinematic point of view that precedes and transcends cinema is crucial to end-of-world culture. By flirting with visions of the destruction of the world and then its heroic salvation, cinematic narratives create a point of view, a "we" who watches most of the earth succumb to destruction while imagining itself as the heroic and worthy fragment of humanity that saves the day. Not only are most postapocalyptic narratives set in the urban centers of the first world—Los Angeles, London, Manhattan—it is the small pocket of privileged humanity from those cities who, in saving itself, saves the world. The "we" that forms the assumed point of view of postapocalyptic cinema is dynamically redemptive. The "we" that assumes the role of humanity in general is both cause for the world's end and also the only agent capable of saving the world. Perhaps the clearest example of this configuration is *Black*

Panther (Ryan Coogler, 2018), where "our" world (the United States) is the destructive other to Wakanda, and yet Wakanda's destiny is to be saved with the help of "us." Once saved, the hero of Wakanda will journey to the United States to save the world from itself. Wakanda is a technologically advanced world that has closed itself off from the violence and imperialism of the globe, yet this isolationism is challenged when an exile threatens Wakanda and is then vanquished with the help of a white CIA agent. The modern imperial fantasy of colonization that looks upon the new world as innocently paradisiacal and yet in need of humanization is only slightly transformed in twenty-first-century dramas of saving the world. The new innocent world does appear to rebuke humanity with its peace and nonacquisitive prosperity, and yet this new world somehow requires the intrusion and salvation of the very humanity that is its threat.

James Cameron's *Avatar* (2009) and George Miller's *Mad Max: Fury Road* (2015) set a world of plunder and hyperconsumption against quasi-Indigenous ecocollectives; these threatened other worlds nevertheless seem to exist to save, and be saved by, *us*. This repeated drama of, at once, recognizing the violence of who we are while constantly replaying our salvation raises a fundamental existential question. Faced with the end of the world, while recognizing that it is *we* who are part of a world destined to end, all we can do is hold on to who we are. Would it be possible to imagine other forms of narrative, those that affirmed the end of who we are—the end of the world—for the sake of something imagined to be less violent and yet *not us*? Throughout this book, I will be using the word "we" in a quite specific and problematic sense; it is the assumed "we" of both postapocalyptic cinema and the assumed "we" of the related sense of the end of the world. To imagine the world ending is to imagine an end to *us*. It is to see other forms of living—even those that seem blissful—as *not us*.

We have plundered the earth, laid waste to the planet by way of centuries of colonialism, slavery, genocide, holocaust, and other barbarisms (with the "we" here becoming increasingly shrill). Yet in the face of the destruction of this all-too-fallen world, the response seems to be—in film after film, novel after novel, and in much of what has come to be known as the environmental humanities—that for all the ills of the past and all the horrors of the present, the world needs to be saved. The violence of the past may be lamentable, but *it's not the end of the world*. Indeed, the destructive nature of the past seems to generate a more intense desire to save the future. Vanquishing what we happen to have been will *and must* bring forth a new and brighter humanity. The event of destruction will bring us together, allow us to recognize and affirm who we are and ought to be. This conception of history—that a fallen present leads to a felicitous future—has a long theological, then liberal, and then posthuman history. It is because the world is *not* paradise that one must either imagine a higher world that would render this life tolerable or imagine that one might finally achieve a less than damaged life in the future.

The long history of theodicy poses the question of how a world created by a just God can contain so much evil. One of the more canonical arguments in favor of theodicy came from Gottfried Wilhelm Leibniz, who, in this *Theodicy* of 1710, argued that God created the best of all possible worlds. Yes, Leibniz conceded, there are some evils, but they are the minimum required in a world of good and freedom.[6] Leibniz was asking the question from the point of view of theology: How could a just God have created a world in which evil exists? But theodicy goes beyond theology and continues into the twenty-first century: How can one justify the evil of this world? Sophocles (496 BC–406 BC) argued that it was better never to have been, a phrase that became the title for the antinatalist philosopher

David Benatar's 2006 book, *Better Never to Have Been*.[7] There is a difference between questioning the "harm" of human existence as such (to use Benatar's phrase) and questioning the justice of *this world*, which was Leibniz's concern. What Leibniz sought to defend was the way this actual world and its specific history had played out rather than human existence, or the civilizing mission that referred to itself as humanity. Yet when Leibniz asks about the world and concludes that we live in the best of all possible worlds, he does so with a sense of the whole of life as a historical totality. One could only pose *this* question, of the value of *this world*, once the modern sense of global humanity had come into play and once there was a sense of world history, of a humanity in general that forms something like a world that we all share.

This sense of world—as a horizon shared by one human community—is what makes the "end of the world" possible. In 1755, forty-five years after Leibniz wrote his *Theodicy*, the city of Lisbon suffered from an earthquake that killed tens of thousands of individuals. The event had a philosophical significance only because news of the destruction traveled beyond the city itself; it was perhaps the first globally broadcast catastrophe. For centuries, there had been accounts and journals of plague, as if one's world might come to an end, but it was the Lisbon earthquake that presented the sudden destruction of modern urban life as the end of *the world*. Global trade and the exchange of information would increasingly allow catastrophes to be world events and to be experienced from afar. If the world's disasters and evils allowed many to question whether there was a God at all, this still left the question of how humans could proceed in a world of so much loss and suffering.[8] This was why, for Kant, theodicy would become a *practical* question that did not concern justifying a God whom we could not possibly know but instead how we as beings of this world could cope with its apparent injustice. For Kant, the idea of global justice is subjective and reflective, a way of viewing the world *as if* it were progressing toward peace. This rendering practical of world justification anticipates the therapeutic and affective narratives of modernity. From a Stoic or tragic acceptance of the contingency of existence, or a more spiritual sense of one's own existence as a mere fragment of a cosmos, the modern project of theodicy assumes that one's own life must make sense in terms of who *we* are. If Leibniz could argue that this was the best of all possible worlds, that was because it was assumed that there was a single world and not, for example, the history of the West and then *other* possible moral and political trajectories. It is the sense of *the world* that makes possible both a question of the justifiability of this world and eventually the end of the world.

In 1784 Kant argued that even though looking back on human history might give one a sense of unreason and barbarism, one ought to proceed *as if* humanity were heading toward perpetual peace and rational cosmopolitanism; however unjustifiable the world may appear to have been, we can, and should, act as if rationality will triumph. This assumption by Kant is, I will argue, cinematic and postapocalyptic. The only way, it seems, to live in this world is to imagine its eventually redeemed future; and the only way that redemption is possible is somehow to look at history and declare that where humanity is at present is not who *we* really are:

> It is admittedly a strange and at first sight absurd proposition to write a *history* according to an idea of how world events must develop if they are to conform to certain rational ends; it would seem that only a *novel* could result from such premises. Yet if it may be assumed that nature does not work without a plan and purposeful end, even amidst the arbitrary play of human freedom, this idea might nevertheless prove useful.

And although we are too short-sighted to perceive the hidden mechanism of nature's scheme, this idea may yet serve as a guide to us in representing an otherwise planless *aggregate* of human actions as conforming, at least when considered as a whole, to a *system*. For if we start out from *Greek* history as that in which all other earlier or contemporary histories are preserved or at least authenticated, if we next trace the influence of the Greeks upon the shaping and mis-shaping of the body politic of *Rome*, which engulfed the Greek state, and follow down to our own times the influence of Rome upon the *Barbarians* who in turn destroyed it, and if we finally add the political history of other peoples *episodically*, in so far as knowledge of them has gradually come down to us through these enlightened nations, we shall discover a regular process of improvement in the political constitutions of our continent (which will probably legislate eventually for all other continents). Furthermore, we must always concentrate our attention on civil constitutions, their laws, and the mutual relations among states, and notice how these factors, by virtue of the good they contained, served for a time to elevate and glorify nations (and with them the arts and sciences). Conversely, we should observe how their inherent defects led to their overthrow, but in such a way that a germ of enlightenment always survived, developing further with each revolution, and prepared the way for a subsequent higher level of improvement.[9]

There have been a few attempts to explain the contradiction between the apparent horror of history and the assumption of humanity's absolute right to life. Kant's argument that despite appearances, we should regard history *as if* it were tending toward peace and felicity was more cautious than the far more recent claims that history *is* actually seeing the triumph of humanity's angelic side and that we have reached the end of ideology to arrive at global self-recognition.[10] Where Kant, the prior history of theodicy, and postapocalyptic cinema differ from a simple affirmation of what Luce Irigaray referred to as "felicity in history" is that rather than simply affirming progress, there was a confrontation with the problem of how on earth we might have a right to a future given the seeming barbarism of the past.[11]

One of the most intriguing articulations of this question of humanist theodicy was Joseph Conrad's *Heart of Darkness* of 1899, which worked with the assumed "we" of humanity, adopting the voice of colonizing rationalization. Well before its cinematic adaptation in Francis Ford Coppola's *Apocalypse Now* (1979), there was something highly cinematic about Conrad's novel, as it pans from an opening scene on London's Thames to journey up the Belgian Congo. When the novel's narrator reflects upon the apparent barbarism of a history of colonialism that does not withstand scrutiny but that can be saved by an idea, he uses a visual metaphor: looking *too closely* at the civilizing mission can only make it appear unjustifiable. What can save the project is some organizing idea—and it is *that* grand idea of humanity as a project that will frame and silence the horror of the details. The narrator of *Heart of Darkness* looks at Marlow telling his tale, as if he were a guru—someone whose wisdom might be transformative—and it is Marlow who offers a vague difference between the apparent and close-range violence of empire versus some idea that might justify the wreckage of history. Marlow draws a distinction between us—we who are efficient and have some ideal—and those other blundering colonizers:

> What saves us is efficiency—the devotion to efficiency. But these chaps were not much account, really. They were no colonists; their administration was merely a squeeze, and

nothing more, I suspect. They were conquerors, and for that you want only brute force—nothing to boast of, when you have it, since your strength is just an accident arising from the weakness of others. They grabbed what they could get for the sake of what was to be got. It was just robbery with violence, aggravated murder on a great scale, and men going at it blind—as is very proper for those who tackle a darkness. The conquest of the earth, which mostly means the taking it away from those who have a different complexion or slightly flatter noses than we, is not a pretty thing when you look into it too much. What redeems it is the idea only. An idea at the back of it; not a sentimental pretense but an idea; and an unselfish belief in the idea—something you can set up, and bow down before, and offer a sacrifice to.[12]

Heart of Darkness places the barbarism of colonization in the background and allows racial dehumanization to be an object of fascination and an occasion for the reflection upon who we are at the end of the world. The text is about the voice of anti-Blackness and its constitutive role in the formation of the civilized "we." *Heart of Darkness* was composed in a milieu concerned with the end of the world. Not only was there a sense of the decline of the West; there was also an articulation of a tendency toward self-destruction in the very potentials of European civilization. To some extent, the notion that reason is threatened from within was central to the Western tradition, where becoming human would be defined as a struggle against unreason—a struggle that was often interpreted using metaphors of slavery. Jean-Jacques Rousseau would refer to being born free but being everywhere in chains,[13] and William Blake described "mind-forg'd manacles."[14] Even though such metaphors suggested self-enslavement, the problem of self-loss was ultimately technological. The external forces that make knowledge and complex societies possible can also rob life of its force and immediacy. In European modernism, one of the technologies perceived as a possible threat to civilization was the archive itself. Without history, civilizations have no sense of who or what they stand for, and yet the texts that grant a culture distinction might circulate as so much noise. Bernard Stiegler referred to the external supports of memory—such as writing, cave painting, and everyday artifacts—as *pharmakon*.[15] Humans become who they are through developing complex relations of memory and desire that transcend the life of individual bodies, but the external storage of these memories also poses the risk of subjection. Norms of art and civility that produce expansion and collective investments in who we are might also become—to use Marlow's phrase from *Heart of Darkness*—"something you can set up, and bow down before, and offer a sacrifice to."

It makes sense that works written within Western culture reflect upon who we are and produce a narrative and reflective community that focuses on what barbarism has done *to us*. Prior to *Heart of Darkness*, there had been centuries of British writing that had argued for the ways in which slavery destroyed and imprisoned the soul of those who were doing the enslaving; far less attention was paid to those enslaved. By the twentieth century, this sense that we are destroyed by the barbarism we inflict on others produced a unified sense of *the world* and its coming to an end. Edmund Husserl diagnosed a crisis in European thought, where technologies of thinking (such as mathematics and geometry) had lost their relation to originating truth and had become merely technical systems;[16] Martin Heidegger followed Husserl in criticizing the tendency for knowledge and thinking to become nothing more than logic.[17] To see the trajectory of Western reason falling into laziness and losing all relation to its origin was a defining feature of European high modernism. The end of the world was often quite explicitly the end of the Western world. This fall would be brought about by the technological drive of the West, not just the machine technologies of industrialization and dehumanization but also the same grand archive of ideas and spirit that produced who we are. The destruction that so concerned modernism came from within the West itself—the desired destruction of the dead weight of the past that would require culture's revivification (Heidegger's *Destruktion* or Ezra Pound's breaking of iambic pentameter) was a response to the West's own trajectory of forgetting and paralysis.[18]

When Conrad looks upon Kurtz in *Heart of Darkness* as the culmination of European learning, there is at one and the same time a dimension of irony—as it is the easily gulled Marlow who deems Kurtz to be so magnificent—accompanied by a critical and ruthless gaze upon the West's will to power. *Heart of Darkness* is both postapocalyptic and cinematic in its narration of the West's internal tendency toward decline from a point of view of global survey, where the Belgian Congo becomes a metaphor and symptom for civilization's essential barbarism. *Heart of Darkness* allows reflection upon who *we* are to take on a global scale that is nevertheless stunningly parochial; those who suffer from the grand idea of the West become nothing more than a backdrop. The terror of civilization captured in Kurtz's final imperative, "Exterminate all the Brutes," has an ambivalence that captures the cinematic myopia of what will become twentieth-century globalism. The drive to extermination may be essential to the very idea of the West, and yet all that remains is a capacity to gaze upon the horror—as if that event alone created sufficient distance. To look upon who we are and weep generates the beautiful soul of the contemporary cinematic subject.

What happens when centuries of seeing ourselves as beset with dangers encounters planetary catastrophe? The metaphysical end of the world meets the physical end of the world: an aesthetic and philosophical tradition that had used figures of destruction, enslavement, and barbarism to describe the capacity for reason to fall back into a brutality that had always been imagined as an external darkness finds itself heading toward a world of resource depletion, systemic collapse, and a brutishness that can no longer be exterminated. *Heart of Darkness* is a telling and diagnostic document; written in an age of mourning for the decline of the West in its moral sense, the novel was one of many texts that started to look upon the documents of civilization as bound up with barbarism. In so doing, though, these critical voices created a presupposed "we" at the end of the world. *Heart of Darkness* is about *us*; it produces a "we" that is at once guilty of empire and yet considers other worlds as so much collateral damage. The same would be true of the novel's film adaptation, *Apocalypse Now*, which repeated the moral tragedy of nearly every U.S. film about the Vietnam War: what is lost and mourned is *our* illusion of moral grandeur. There is neither voice, face, nor vision attributed to *them*. *Heart of Darkness* and *Apocalypse Now* are about the end of the world insofar as they confront the end of the grand lie of civilization. They are also texts that produce the end of the world as the end of *us*, or—more accurately—the end of us as the end of the world.

The narrative arc of *Heart of Darkness* anticipates twenty-first-century postapocalyptic culture in its focus on our moral bankruptcy, a revelation of emptiness that becomes the occasion for creating a distanced and enlightened "we" that can look upon the horrors of the past with the knowledge that we— in this very act of viewing—might be other than the empire that has made our very condition of viewing possible. Like *Apocalypse Now*, *Heart of Darkness* sees the tragedy of empire and racism as an indictment of *us* and in so doing creates a point of view from which we might examine our lesser selves. It is as though there were *only* this "we" of a lamentable past and a fragile future. Of course, there are non-Hollywood and non-Western contributions to the thought of the end of the world, but it is Hollywood cinema's structure of surveying a past of violence while affirming a future of humanity that is both dominant and typical of a humanist culture that extends well beyond cinema and popular culture.

Right to Life

The question of how Western humanity can claim an absolute right to life despite its history of barbarism rarely gets asked but is nevertheless constantly answered. End-of-world cinema is an occasion for affirming that whatever else happens, however fragile and guilty we may happen to be, *we must survive*. Even more importantly, it is because the past has been so destructive that there must be a future of redemption. The less-than-just past is frequently depicted as leading necessarily to a future that allows humanity to become the moral being it has always imagined itself to be. On the one hand, this ties in with a traditional sense of apocalyptic revelation that will slough off the corruption of the present in order to disclose a higher truth; on the other hand, what is revealed in postapocalyptic culture is nothing more than an intensification of *who we are*. Historical narratives—especially as they are rendered into shape for Hollywood cinema—often take the redemptive and performative form of finding humanity in a trail of wreckage. The "we" who can gaze with horror at the narrow-minded and brutal past is produced through affective distancing; the tears of sentiment that flow when we mourn the past produce a righteous subject of the present.[19]

By looking on the past as a less enlightened era of racism, anti-Semitism, homophobia, transphobia, or some other form of narrow-mindedness, we become an expansive and empathetic moral subject of the present. One of the clearest examples is Steven Spielberg's 1993 *Schindler's List* (based on Thomas Keneally's 1982 *Schindler's Ark*)—somehow the Nazi extermination of millions of Jews becomes a heartwarming tale about one man's resistance. Oscar Schindler's saving of a very few lives becomes a way of affirming humanity in general, with the Holocaust then becoming something we can look upon as in the past and as being at odds with who we are. Such narratives have the same performative force of more explicitly end-of-world narratives: we in the present can feel the horror of what we once were, feeling a loss and sadness of the past that enables the future to meekly inherit the earth. *Boys Don't Cry* (Kimberly Pierce, 1999) situates small-town transphobia in the rural past; *Brokeback Mountain*'s (Ang Lee, 2005) tale of love in a homophobic backwater is set in the sixties; *Green Book* (Peter Farrelly, 2018), like *Schindler's List*, places prejudice in the past but also charts the redemption of one white crusader as he learns to overcome his racism and homophobia (attributed to his Italian immigrant small-mindedness, while his wife bears all the female virtues of empathy). The problem with such redemption narratives is the assumption of a naturally moral humanity that is inevitably white, Western, and progressive (because the future is always more promising), despite all the evidence put forward by the same narratives. How is it that tales of slavery, genocide, racism, and extermination nevertheless contribute to humanism's assumed right to life? They do so by being both situated in the past or elsewhere and—by way of narration and point of view—split off from who we properly are. Telling a story about a past and an elsewhere creates a "we" of the present able to gaze with horror at that other not-yet-human humanity of the past.

The "we" of this humanity is produced from a series of splits: between past and future, between the stateless and the rich in world, and between highly individuated humans blessed with a sense of humanity as a virtual ideal and those whom this elevated humanity can recognize, even if they don't yet have a sense of themselves as human. The liberal subject of the ideal future is, Francis Fukuyama has suggested, "the last man."[20] He—and it is a "he"—is no longer attached to a specific mode of existence and is capable of recognizing humanity in all its variants as nothing other than a capacity for self-formation; this exemplary "last man" looks on others with recognition, even if those others have not yet made that same passage to liberal autonomy. This is not just a philosophical motif; it structures the "we" of what has come to be called the Anthropocene. Even if the destruction of the planet was caused by Western capitalism, the language of the future assumes a common predicament that affects us all and generates a single horizon for redemption.

By the twenty-first century, we recognize humans as a species capable of transforming the earth as a living system. The event of recognition is itself productive of a "we." Earth has been damaged by the human species; therefore, humanity counts as a single agent. The hyperconsuming and media-rich West looks upon the rest of the world as those who will suffer the consequences of a long history of global transformation and charges itself with saving this same world. The formal structure of postapocalyptic cinema—where we are agents, at once, of destruction and of salvation—mirrors the form of Anthropocene discourse. Think tanks and research centers concerned with saving the future of humanity care only to save those humans who are tending toward technological maturity and superintelligence. To lose many humans would be lamentable, but to lose intelligence would be the end of the world.[21] In postapocalyptic cinema, the planet as a whole is often threatened with destruction, and yet it is a small group of humans surveying, saving, and managing the world who are at the center of the narrative and who also emerge as the heroes and masters of the future. This narrative and cinematic production of a presupposed "we" with an absolute right to life is symptomatic of, and essential for, the ongoing species split that marks the discourses of humanism. The "Anthropos" of the Anthropocene is not the species as a whole; instead, the species is split between those who manage and survey the planet, recognizing and affirming itself as "humanity," and those background "others" who may or may not be saved. To take just one example, *Independence Day* (Roland Emmerich, 1996) sees the entire globe threatened with alien invasion. Not only is the battle to vanquish the aliens waged from the central command of the United States, but the final victory also sees July 4 as a day of global recognition and freedom. The heroic overcoming of a possible end of the world by some humans generates a new and brighter future, where we are now one. In the end, all the world will be America.

Humanity

This book is, ostensibly, about postapocalyptic cinema; but its broader focus is on the cinematic nature of what has come to be called humanity and the presupposed "we" of humanity and humanism. Not only does postapocalyptic cinema present humanity by way of highly specific and contracted figures of who we supposedly are; it also intensifies a much longer tradition of exemplary humanism that has always been concerned with saving the world. Well before the explicit world-saving dramas of Hollywood blockbusters, there has been a much longer political, philosophical, literary, and theological history that depicts the very depletion of the world as the occasion for its redemption. It is because we are in the worst of all possible worlds that there *must be* a better future. Dystopia inevitably leads to the entitlement of humanity to inherit the future. Rather than centuries of imperialism, slavery, colonization, war, and genocide leading to a resignation that the world was bound to end, the intensification of destruction generates an imperative that the new world will finally arrive. Well before the efflorescence of postapocalyptic culture in the twenty-first century, there had been an intrinsically apocalyptic tendency in humanist thought: whatever humanity happens to be will fall away as humanity arrives at its promise, with a radical bifurcation occurring between the tragic past and the blessed future. The apparently destructive and fallen nature of the world is not at all evidence of humanity's unworthiness but is rather its entitlement to the future. We must live on to triumph over all that we have been for the sake of who we really are.

The "we" of this existential predicament is produced through the time of this entitlement. Only those blessed with the liberal-Christian-humanist sense of beatitude can recognize the past as a fall away from humanity's proper potential; suffering from who we are allows us to inherit the future. Either this can take the form of the disciplinary recognition of geologists, anthropologists, and political theorists, who argue that the "Anthropos" that has inflicted planetary damage is now a geological agent to be reckoned with and whose effected unity must now be held responsible for the future, *or* it can take the more mythic form where looking at a world on the brink of destruction produces an overwhelming sense of a right to life. Humanity, in recognizing itself as a global force, becomes too big to fail. Disciplinary and academic examples of this right to life constituted through planetary damage include conceptions of the "good Anthropocene" (where the power to destroy the planet indicates a power of future restoration) and less Promethean demands that accept the volatility of the Anthropocene.[22] Clive Hamilton is critical of the arrogance of those who would deploy science to maintain the attachment to expansion; his questioning of the drama of an indomitable humanity nevertheless, and understandably, takes the form of adjusting *our* grand narrative: "As the basis for our deepest social structures, as well as our individual understandings of our own futures, the destabilization of the narrative calls everything into question. The direction in which we thought we were going has now been denied to us. The historical force of this should not be missed, for it means that the utopian promise of all political and religious ideologies, both materialist and metaphysical, vanishes."[23] This "we" of the Anthropocene who admits guilt but nevertheless takes charge of the future not only is characteristic of forms of theory that assume a single historical agent but also marks forms of literature that see climate change as a "wake up call." One question raised in the chapters that follow is whether—as Hamilton suggests—*all* promise vanishes; could it be that there is plenty of promise but not for *us*? This is not just to say that the future might belong to someone other than the threatened man of reason whose embattled history promises that he will ultimately inherit the earth; it is also to question the axiology of the end of the world. First, what is depicted as the end of the world—from the point of view of privileged affluence—frequently mirrors the forms of life that the West deems to be inhuman: conditions of indentured labor, resource depletion, statelessness, and intense vulnerability. Second, such conditions—despite being depicted as what we must avoid—are demanded of those others whom we also seek to save. Third, are these end-of-world scenarios of statelessness, loss of global interconnectedness, and mere subsistence really the end of the world?

One common narrative structure of postapocalyptic cinema is to depict a dystopian future that is a likely fulfilment of our current trajectory; and then from this moment of utter depletion, the same world that was lost is saved and redeemed. This is perhaps what makes twenty-first-century culture *post*apocalyptic; after the end, there will be no new world, only a yearning to make the world great again, returning to humanism in a heightened form. The very anthropos who brought the world to an end will save the world, regaining humanity in a purified and hyperhumanist form. Nowhere is this more apparent than in *Blade Runner 2049*. It is now unremarkable for end-of-world narratives to open on a future of desolation; no reason needs to be given. (Cormac McCarthy's *The Road* [2006] simply assumes this end, giving no suggestion of how life contracted to nothing more than bare human existence.) In *Blade Runner 2049* the future is in the hands of a biotech monopoly, with the only rupture of control possible being the capacity for replicants to reproduce miraculously. If dystopia is a world in which technology has displaced us, then the only utopia imaginable is a retrieval of us, in the narrowest of familial forms. *Blade Runner 2049* sees the central character searching for the man whom he believes to be his biological father, as though this alone could grant his life authenticity and promise a future of humanity in its proper (biologically reproductive) form. Rather than a better version of a technology-enhanced future, the only imaginable ideal after the end of the world is the return of human birth. As in so many postapocalyptic dramas, it is the retrieval of the family that offers hope.

What Lee Edelman refers to as "reproductive futurism" takes an intensified form in postapocalyptic culture.[24] The figure of the child enables the future of humanity to appear as an innocent potentiality—not what humanity is and has been but what it ought to be. As long as there are children, there is always hope that the future may be different from its less than perfect actuality and history. One stunning example from postapocalyptic cinema is *The Day the Earth Stood Still* (Scott Derrickson, 2008), where aliens arrive to save the earth *from humans*. The narrative arc dogmatically assumes the immorality of the aliens' task; destroying us in the name of some supposed higher (inhuman) justice is prima facie evil—evil *because* it is not us. The human right to life is "justified" solely through a capacity to mourn the past. The film reaches its happy ending when a child weeps for his dead father and, in so doing, convinces the aliens of human value. However destructive humanity may have been at the planetary level, a child's love for his father is enough to restore the right to life. For Edelman, refusing the fetishized figure of the child would force us to confront the impossible and necessary gap between the imaginary conception of humanity and the brute force of the real. How might we think about our world, our polity, if we did not have the child as the presumed restoration of the good? For Edelman, the ideal of a blessed humanity that has a due right to a pure and justified future falls apart once one subtracts the figure of the child. In addition to Edelman's critique of reproductive futurism—which is focused on the ways in which the heteronormativity of the family occludes the structural violence of the polity—Rebekah Sheldon has tied the figure of the child to specifically ecological forms of redemption. Saving the world for our children is yet one more way in which the world and its future is bound intimately to *us*. Sheldon's *The Child to Come* looks at the ways in which the imagined child who inherits the earth precludes the possibility of thinking about radically different futures; what is desired and imagined is nothing more than humanity as it is in a purified, moralized, and utterly static mode. Rather than confronting the ways in which everything that has forged itself under the name of humanity contributes to destruction, the figure of the threatened child generates *both* a demand that the world as it is be saved and allows everything other than the innocence of the child to be void of sense and possibility. For Sheldon, both the threatened child *and* the contemplation of destruction "are the twin poles of catastrophic narratives": "The blank face of the child, the blank face of decimation, perfect health or perfect destruction, are preferable to—and modes of controlling—nonrepetitive futures."[25] The only future available is the repetition of who we are, even if the ideal future of who we are requires imagining the destruction of that other portion of humanity that is not quite us. What Sheldon and Edelman focus on is the child as repetition of the same, but what they pay less attention to is the way these same narratives of redemption require the annihilation of an evil other, a *not us*.

What I would add to Edelman's "reproductive futurism" and Sheldon's "reproduction of fixity" is that the future's fixity and sameness is tied to an absolute right to life of a familial "we" that is produced by a predominantly cinematic point of view that gazes upon worldless others. Saving the world and saving the children, who are the idealized humanity of the future world, occurs against a backdrop of so many worldless others. Saving the world does not at all amount to saving the planet but ultimately to saving one's kind, with the force of kindred being produced through visual and disciplinary technologies. The child is, as Edelman and Sheldon recognize, a way of imagining the future as an innocent repetition of the present, but it is also more specifically one's *own* present. "The" child is always a child of one's own. Saving the world amounts to not only saving one's own self and one's own kind but also allowing—and often enjoying—the destruction of anything or anyone *not* oneself. Saving humanity really amounts to saving *us*.

Crucial to this structure is the narrative and cinematic technology of point of view; we follow a subject whose task it is to save the world, watching most of the earth either die or become inhuman, with humanity in its closed familial form inheriting the future. In *I Am Legend* the border between "us" and "them" is played out in a narrative trajectory that increasingly becomes a limit of simple recognition. There is much one could say about the metaphysical conundrum of zombies—those beings who are "us" but without the interiority or sense of self that constitutes being human. Twenty-first-century zombie fiction has often meditated on this strange border of becoming *not us*. Colson Whitehead's 2011 novel *Zone One*—like so many postapocalyptic dramas—is set in Manhattan. In addition to the walking dead, there are also barely moving bodies trapped in their past attachments. Like the later *Severance* (2018) by Ling Ma, *Zone One* suggests that there was already an undead quality to affluent urbanity, so that the zombification of who we are simply intensifies an unthought self-attachment. Zombie narratives are always more or less critical explorations of the problem of holding on to who we are. The zombie is clearly *not us*, allowing the difference between human and inhuman to be defined as the absence or presence of self-consciousness, while the liminal figures are those who appear to be as we once were. They are "us" but without future. When white colonizers depicted Indigenous peoples, they did so with the gaze that *Zone One* imagines one directs toward zombies; they are "us" but without a sense of being us, without time and futurity. *I Am Legend*'s entire trajectory turns on this border. Prior to the film's spectacular ending, the central character's dog is bitten. Nursing his dog, Robert Neville (Will Smith) notices the first signs of the dog becoming a zombie and at that moment kills the canine whom he loves before she becomes *one of them*. In the final stages of the film, Neville is separated from the zombies by a glass wall while holding the vaccine that could help them once again become human—become like him. As zombies, however, they have no interest in being him. Being human only has value if you are human. Failing to convince the zombies that they could give up being who they are—which would amount to giving up being without a sense of who they are—Neville passes the vaccine to a mother and child who will travel to what's left of humanity and thereby allow Neville's own kind to continue.

After killing his sole companion at the moment his dog begins to show signs of becoming one of them, Neville sacrifices his own life for the sake of a humanity to come, as mother and child head to New Hampshire. Neville may have lost his own family prior to being the last man residing in Manhattan, but it is the family in general he saves by handing the vaccine to the mother and child. If the figure of the child allows the future to be imagined as the continuation of the present, it is the figure of the family, and especially the father who gives his life for his family, that brings to the fore an essential element of the postapocalyptic imaginary. It is not simply that the future is the continuity and redemption of the present but also that there is an ongoing calculation of how much one is willing to lose or sacrifice in order to be oneself. What would you do and who would you kill to save the world?

In a zombie epic such as *I Am Legend*, the clear creation of a point of view of an "us" that is threatened by *them* generates a heroic narrative drive where *they* must be destroyed in order for the world to be saved; if this means that one must kill those of us who become other, suddenly zombified, then so be it. Saving the world may amount to sacrificing one's life, but one would do so in order to avoid us all becoming like them. Ultimately, as *I Am Legend* makes all too clear, simply staying alive or saving life is not at all what matters; it must be *our* life. Better to die in the name of saving humanity than allow the world to be nothing more than *them*.

The species bifurcation that is so heavily marked in zombie cinema—between a "we" of self-consciousness and a mere object "them"—is structural to end-of-world cinema in general. The "we" who can gaze upon and recognize others, while looking at those same others with pity and desire, is constitutive of the humanism surrounding the future of humanity. It is not just that the world that is saved is ours but more importantly that our world is the *only* human world. This highly normative and cinematic conception of humanity relies heavily on both the nuclear family as the basic social unit from which legitimate polities are composed *and* a subject blessed with the global media and network capacities to survey the world from the privacy and safety of their own space. The only world worth saving is this world that unfolds from the secure space of individual survey; a nonfamilial, tribal, or nomadic world is no world at all. The heroism of save-the-world narratives is frequently intertwined with a subplot of familial redemption; this enables a division between the generic world that is saved and the world that matters—the world of the nuclear family. Neville's sacrifice in *I Am Legend* is one of many fatherly gestures of heroism that allow the life of one's own kind to be worth killing and dying for. In Christopher Nolan's *Interstellar* (2014), set in a future of resource depletion, the father must choose between sacrificing humanity as it is (including his own family) for the sake of the species' future and saving the life of his own family. Would you allow all you know and love to die for the sake of saving your own kind? This question posed in *Interstellar* is at the heart of humanity and its various discourses of humanism. We must live on, and we must make sacrifices in order to do so, but the calculation is always an economy of *us*. *We are this economy*: ongoing death for the sake of *our* life. Heroically refusing the deal that would require him to abandon the earth in order to secure humanity's future, *Interstellar*'s hero manages to travel through time and save present humanity for the future (all with the help of his own child speaking to him from the future that he saved). A similar trope structures *Everything Everywhere All at Once*. The mother refuses to sacrifice her daughter for the sake of the universe, but this refusal ultimately restores her and her family *and*, in doing so, saves the world as we know it. It would be intolerable to have to lose one's own kind for the sake of an abstraction, even if that abstraction is humankind or even life in general. This is because humanity is never truly abstract but is always a generalization of familial "man." One would die to save one's own and would kill all that is not one's own, but dying and killing for something as abstract as humanity or life is unbearable. It must be *our* humanity that survives. Postapocalyptic dramas that ostensibly concern saving the world usually harbor an underlying question of just who counts as worthy of saving, and this question frequently requires a child who is one's own.

While the child is a figure for a future of pure promise, not yet sullied by what humanity has been, it is often the father's sacrifice and redemption in a familial narrative that is bound up with securing the child's future. In Roland Emmerich's *2012* (2009), Jackson Curtis (John Cusack) learns of the impending destruction of the earth, along with a government plot to save the elite by building planetary arks—what Dipesh Chakrabarty referred to as "lifeboats for the rich."[26] The highly moralized binary structure of the narrative pits an evil government seeking to save humanity in some general administrative form against the good father seeking to save his family, from whom—up until this point—he has been estranged. *His* saving of the world is not at all the calculating utilitarian selection of the world's elites but is focused first on those who are his own. This then leads to a good saving of the world—not a mere calculus but a redemption by way of parochial attachments. The father who had abandoned his family for the sake of the world (being too focused on the general good of his career) returns to save his family and in so doing saves the true and better world. Good and evil, here as elsewhere, can be mapped onto the parochial versus the general.

Fatherly sacrifice and redemption also feature heavily in *Independence Day*, exposing the intimate tie between the family, the assumption of who we are, and the intertwining of America with the morality of kindred. I deliberately use the term "America" here in the same way that I use the term "humanity": when actions are referred to as "un-American" or when appeals are made to make "America" great again, there is a synecdoche at work. America is not the United States but a certain highly colonized imagination of a "New World." In the same way, humanity is not the human species but an idealized contraction. When the world as a whole is threatened, and there appears to be a utilitarian problem of whether one saves humanity in general or those to whom one is immediately attached, it is the familial drama that restores coherence. One's family turns out to be the fragment of humanity that restores the whole. Saving one's own kind amounts to saving the world, with the redemption of the family and the father coinciding with the emergence of a new world. In *Independence Day* the U.S. president (Bill Pullman), a champion fighter pilot (Will Smith), and a fallen MIT graduate reduced to working for a cable company (Jeff Goldblum) join forces to defeat an alien invasion, with their heroism restoring their familial ties, while also allowing America's July 4 to become a day of global freedom. As with *Interstellar* and *2012*, fathers who fall on hard times pave the way for familial reconciliation that is bound up with world restoration. The homely bourgeois man whose civic duty tears him away from a private sphere in an increasingly corporate and disenchanted world is given an opportunity to become a global hero and return to his rightful place in the bourgeois private sphere. The man of reason and duty who would sacrifice his own life, and all those not his own, enables the child to inherit the future. All these tales of saving the world are moral fables that split the species in two—between the purely calculative sense of the species as a whole and the sentimental and *properly human* saving of one's own. Saving the world appears as an imperative only insofar as it is saving *us*.

In *Black Panther* the technologically advanced and peace-ful utopia of Wakanda appears to have arrived at the form of political maturity dreamed of by Western liberalism; the social whole is cohesive, compassionate, and unhindered by drives for expansion. The narrative begins with this bounded equilibrium being threatened by one of Wakanda's own; an American-exiled lost son faces off with Wakanda's rightful heir and leader. In a narrative that pits the technological and moral sophistication of Wakanda against the corruption of a fallen America, it is nevertheless America that is recognized as worthy of redemp-tion in the film's conclusion. Wakanda's hero awakens from his isolationist and utopian slumbers to take on the duty of saving America, with Wakanda itself vanquishing its intrud-ers with the help of a white CIA agent. A brief idealization of non-Western cultures is followed by a recognition that any such imaginable others would, ultimately, step in to save (and be saved by) white America.

In a similar manner, James Cameron's *Avatar* (2009) depicts an idyllic, ecologically attuned, and resource-rich land of Pandora, which is threatened with invasion by a militaristic and plun-dering U.S. military. Pandora valiantly wins its heroic battle of resistance but only (again) with the help of virtuous Americans who are able to attune themselves to Pandora's moral value. Even these enclosed utopias recognize, and require, the saving force of American heroism. Both *Avatar* and *Black Panther* depict worlds threatened by humanity (America) in its violent and life-denying forms but then are saved when that same America finds in the new world its better self. What marks out this species bifurcation—between the rapacious humanity that has been and the just humanity to come—is a certain form of *owness*. Both *Avatar* and *Black Panther* begin by posing utopian worlds that are *not us*. Why would we not allow the narrative to take the form of annihilating the intrusive and dystopian other that is, at least from the film's point of view, initially us? These begin as reverse alien-invasion films—we are the aliens threatening to destroy a peaceful and stable world. Gradually, the narrative point of view shifts to the world of the other, who then also becomes us, as we allow that world to be saved, sloughing off the old and destructive "we" of the past.

Humanity as Such

At the heart of the concept of saving the world is a necessary and apocalyptic sacrifice. Saving the world is unquestionably always saving who we are, but this requires deciding on who we *properly are*. Not only are we not *them*; it is often the case that the end of others' lives is more than collateral damage. It is the annihilation of *them* that affirms who we are.

In a manner that is similar to *The Day the Earth Stood Still*, George Nolfi's *The Adjustment Bureau* (2011) features managerial aliens who tell humans that their obviously destructive history forfeits all rights to future freedom. Despite the aliens' claim to be adjusting the world for the sake of saving life and avoiding suffering, the film's narrative turns on the redemptive power of human fallibility. The aliens who are coming to *save* the earth do so in the name of moral superiority. The bureau's representative explains to the central characters (two lovers) that there have been two occasions when the world was allowed to proceed without adjustment; this resulted in the Dark Ages and the Holocaust. Even so, the film affirms the beauty and contingency of human love (in the form of the heterosexual couple) over the ruthless and managerial "adjustment" of human affairs for the sake of avoiding violence. This is how theodicy has always operated—violence is the price we pay for this free world of ours. The 1962 series of *The Twilight Zone* featured an episode "To Serve Man." Technologically advanced aliens invade a crisis-ridden earth and at first appear to be doing all that is required to save the earth and serve man. After enabling world peace and allowing humans to travel back to the aliens' own planet, the content of their manifesto, *To Serve Man*, is finally translated and turns out to be a cookbook. The episode is a tale of horror; another species' technological and moral maturity is, from our point of view, not at all a right to destroy and consume *us*. This is, though, how humanity has defined itself: intelligent and technologically mature to the point of being able to kill and consume those beings who are *not us*.

Our commitment to saving the world of humanity is not grounded in some absolute value regarding who we are but is a parochial attachment to *us*, and it turns out that if we imagine enhanced versions of who we are trying to take our place, this fills us with horror. This is not because those imagined beings are essentially horrific, for they are simply doing what we do every day: killing and consuming what is required, in order to save the world, and often doing so on the basis of species exceptionalism. When presented with a counterfactual of variously superior aliens—whether Pandora, Wakanda, or technologically advanced extraterrestrials—it seems impossible to accept that we might not possess an absolute right to life. Whatever *their* moral or technological maturity, the horror lies in them being *not us*, an existential relation to otherness that is played out in alien-invasion tales, in spy fiction, and increasingly in postapocalyptic cinema. We might witness vast swathes of the planet fall to destruction, but if that privileged pocket of humanity that is like us manages to survive, then the world has been saved.

Sympathy and Point of View

Nothing seems more urgent than saving the world, as long as that world is ours. The sense of ownness, and the imperative to save what is one's own, is constituted through the possibility of its end. As soon as the world is threatened, its very sense of being both worthy and *ours* becomes ever more intense. All that appears lamentable—all that an imagined superior species might consider worthy of annihilation—suddenly appears worthy in the face of our threatened nonbeing. Narrative and cinematic techniques of point of view are crucial to the technologies of sympathy that attach us to specific worlds. There is no "view from nowhere," but one way to think about modern Western thought is its distinctly personal point of view—tales told from the perspective of a single individual—rather than cosmologies that possess a range that transcends the world. One way of thinking about literature and cinema is that its use of various points of view enables readers and viewers to sympathize with others; there would be something ethical per se about the capacity to imagine living in another's shoes. For philosophers like Martha Nussbaum, literature would be an exercise in sympathy, one that would temper philosophy's tendency toward abstraction.[27] For Nussbaum, literature takes who we are and expands the range of sympathy. Nussbaum is not alone among philosophers and literary critics who pose the problem of expanding the range of sympathy from the individual to distant others.[28] The flagrant parochialism of postapocalyptic culture suggests that we should reverse this relation between sympathy and point of view. Rather than thinking of persons who might consume fictions that enable them to sympathize with others, it is better to think of fictions, figures, symbols, and narratives as constitutive of the points of view or worlds that compose personhood. Persons are the effect of technologies of point of view. Gilles Deleuze, after Leibniz, referred to this as perspectivism—it is from perceptions that a certain world is effected.[29] This does not mean that everything is relative but rather that analysis of the ways in which points of view are assembled opens to a truth beyond the world that is already ours, beyond the lived. What counts as a technology of point of view varies significantly, from speculative, philosophical, religious, and cosmic modes that aim for expansive range to the parochialism that is most clearly on display in postapocalyptic culture. To have a world is to have a point of view, and vice versa. If I can recognize and sympathize with others, this is because I can imagine them, too, as having a range of sympathies and attachments. One dominant understanding of liberalism is dependent on the capacity for any individual to imagine themselves as one of many others, all of whom have their own world.[30] The capacity to recognize others as blessed with their own world and point of view is, however, as much of a contraction as it is an expansion. It narrows point of view to the imaginative subject and imagines sympathy as traveling from one human person to another.

Rather than think of point of view as something from which narration emerges, one might say that point of view emerges from narration and that modes of narration have varying registers, or various ways to mark self and other, inside and outside. Returning to Nussbaum's claim of literature and sympathy, it would make sense to say not only that literature enables a subject to have a sense of another's point of view but also that literary point of view is what brings subjects and sympathy into being, a subject being nothing more than the attachments, relations, and feelings of kindred and collectively formed inscriptions that compose a world.

There are many philosophical, theoretical, anthropological, and political ways in which thinking about point of view helps us to confront the problem of the end of the world and the acute political urgencies that accompany saving the world. Eduardo Viveiros de Castro has been critical of the humanist anthropology that encounters all others as variants of the human, a category that allows the anthropologist to adopt a position of grand interpreter of all other worlds. Viveiros de

Castro describes the anthropologist's subsumption of all possible worlds into variants of the human as parochial when compared to the many and varied Indigenous cosmologies that understand both the relation to others in terms of different modes of personhood and those others as themselves possessing multiple understandings of personhood:

> The ethnography of indigenous America is replete with references to a cosmopolitical theory describing a universe inhabited by diverse types of actants or subjective agents, human or otherwise-gods, animals, the dead, plants, meteorological phenomena, and often objects or artifacts as well-equipped with the same general ensemble of perceptive, appetitive, and cognitive dispositions: with the same kind of soul. This interspecific resemblance includes, to put it a bit performatively, the same mode of apperception: animals and other nonhumans having a soul "see themselves as persons" and therefore "are persons": intentional, double-sided (visible and invisible) objects constituted by social relations and existing under a double, at once reflexive and reciprocal—which is to say collective—pronominal mode. What these persons see and thus are as persons, however, constitutes the very philosophical problem posed by and for indigenous thought.
>
> The resemblance between souls, however, does not entail that what they express or perceive is likewise shared. The way humans see animals, spirits and other actants in the cosmos is profoundly different from how these beings both see them and see themselves. Typically, and this tautology is something like the degree zero of perspectivism, humans will, under normal conditions, see humans as humans and animals as animals (in the case of spirits, seeing these normally invisible beings is a sure indication that the conditions are not normal: sickness, trance and other "altered states"). . . .

All animals and cosmic constituents are intensively and virtually persons because all of them, no matter which, can reveal themselves to be (transform into) a person. This is not a simple logical possibility but an ontological potentiality.[31]

This radical perspectivism places Western humanism and its mode of universalism within the context of a broader universalism. What is the point of view from which the universe is imagined? Is it one in which we are the world and must be saved for the sake of existence in general, or does one imagine the world one inhabits as one expression among many that might bear some relation to a universe of which one is a fragment? The human subject who thinks of ethics as expanding sympathy to include all other humans would be but one mode of speculation; other modes would include, but not be limited to, Indigenous forms of speculation that imagine various nonhumans as blessed with forms of personhood that are not simply lesser versions of one's own. Rather than think of universalism as inclusive, it might be thought of as disjunctive, where it is because I do not recognize you as human like me that you are worthy of regard. It may well be true, as Thomas Nagel has argued, that no amount of information regarding bat consciousness will ever enable us to experience what it is like to be a bat.[32] But we may add to this that even if no amount of knowledge can give us such experience, we nevertheless *do* and *should* strive to think what such worlds might be like. If no amount of knowledge can add up to the experience of being a bat, then the same applies to other persons—human and nonhuman. There is ethical value in imagining other persons, human and nonhuman, and their worlds. But this would only amount to an expanded narcissism if one were not to recognize that the idea we have of other worlds and the ideas those others have of us are not commensurable; nor can they be flattened out to a single and absolute domain of value. No amount of knowledge or sympathy can eliminate the parochialism that we must also, nevertheless, temper with the awareness of a cosmos composed of a thousand tiny parochialisms. The same applies to the parochialism of saving "the" world.

When Steven Jay Gould weighed in on the environmental question of which species, in an age of extinction, ought to be saved, he began by noting the parochial investment in our own species. Gould then went on to note that it would be neither desirable nor plausible to strive for an environmentalism that would freeze evolutionary time and simply save the world we have: "I do not think that, practically or morally, we can defend a policy of saving every distinct local population of organisms. I can cite a good rationale for the preservation of species—for each species is a unique and separate natural object that, once lost, can never be reconstituted. But subspecies are distinct local populations of species with broader geographical ranges. Subspecies are dynamic, interbreedable, and constantly changing; what then are we saving by declaring them all inviolate?"[33] In the case Gould was considering, he decided that we should save the Mount Graham red squirrel because it was of scientific interest for students of evolution and because of its crucial place in the habitat. That second reason would seem to suggest that species ought to be saved for the sake of life, but for Gould this returns us to the parochial interest we have in *human* life: "Capacity for recovery at geological scales has no bearing whatever upon the meaning of extinction today. We are not protecting Mount Graham red squirrels because we fear for global stability in a distant future not likely to include us. We are trying to preserve populations and environments because the comfort and decency of our present lives, and those of fellow species that share our planet, depend upon such stability. Mass extinctions may not threaten distant futures, but they are decidedly unpleasant for species in the throes of their power."[34] Gould goes on to chart a path between an environmentalism that focuses on saving the planet (which he sees as human chauvinism and a disregard for *who* benefits from the environment) and a rampant acceptance of extinction as natural. The point, he argues, is not simply to stop extinction nor to let it run its course but to think about saving ourselves ethically: "We have never entirely shaken this legacy of environmentalism as something opposed to immediate human needs, particularly of the impoverished and unfortunate. But the Third World expands and contains most of the pristine habitat that we yearn to preserve. Environmental movements cannot prevail until they convince people that clean air and water, solar power, recycling, and reforestation are best solutions (as they are) for human needs at human scales—and not for impossibly distant planetary futures."[35] Save the world, save the planet, but don't just save the privileged few, and don't save the planet without thinking of the world's poor. What Gould starts to think about is the dynamic and contested nature of the species that we are parochially invested in: save the world but *don't* save the environment for the sake of privileged enjoyment—save water, save food, save habitats. What makes Gould's intervention compelling is his acceptance of species parochialism, and it is this acceptance that should prompt us to ask both about the human that is so urgently being saved *and* about the very structure of parochial attachments per se. To say that we have a parochial attachment to who we are can apply to our attachment to the species, but it also applies—and this is obvious in postapocalyptic culture—to a far narrower sense of the human that does not include the species as a whole.

Parochialism

I want to pause and reflect on what it means to accept that one has a parochial attachment to one's kind. This is quite different from saying that our existence is necessarily and constitutively normative—rather that the normative and the parochial are intertwined. Rather than think of norms as being in part parochial, it would be more accurate to say that our ways of thinking about norms is highly parochial. Humans often claim to be exceptional and more worthy because, unlike animals, they are normative beings. We might say, and many have, that human existence is worthier of being saved because we are rational, moral, cultural, and technologically advanced beings. We are worthy because we are normative, and *our* norms seem to be properly moral rather than simply consisting of likes and preferences. Our norms are those of rationality, ethics, and aesthetics and not simply the fulfilment of drives. It is both possible and necessary not only to question what counts as reason, morality, and aesthetics, along with the parochialism of being attached to certain traditions and modes of reason, but also to recognize that such elevating norms have supreme value *for us*. Within this species parochialism, there is the further and far less defensible parochialism that attaches to planet-destructive forms of humanism.

Nowhere is this more apparent than in postapocalyptic cinema. Often the postapocalyptic scenario is an all-too-predictable dystopian intensification of the world that has been lost, and yet it is that same world—with all its destructive attachments—that must be saved. *Interstellar* shows a world of resource depletion managed by biopolitical expediency, and yet the heroism of the film is given in the form of a frontier spirit that traverses the cosmos for the sake of saving one's own nuclear family. *Mad Max: Fury Road* begins with the tyranny of a world of scarcity, where the control of water and oil amounts to absolute power. The battle against this tyranny, again, takes the form of the lone male warrior hero who will harness the power of a group of women warriors. The pseudo-Indigenous women's collective offers itself as the future but does so with the help of the male warrior, who is also the fragment of the world that is going to be saved—the warrior spirit who brings humanity in its proper and world-saving form into the future. As with *Black Panther* and *Avatar*, even when the world that is saved is the "new world" (of Black or Indigenous culture), it is the white male hero who saves what then becomes *the* world, "our" world. End-of-world culture is inextricably intertwined with the colonizing imaginary of the new world. On the one hand, colonization cannot recognize those whom it conquers as sufficiently like us to be worthy of being fully human and rich in world, and yet it valorizes the innocence it encounters in the new world in order to forge a fantasy of self-renewal by way of the not-yet-human other. Point of view and its constitutive parochialism operates through twists and turns of annihilation, redemption, fantasy, nostalgia, utopia, world ending, and world saving.

Perhaps one of the most illuminating discussions of point of view and attachment, though it does not use those terms directly, is Christine Korsgaard's work on *our* obligations to other animals. The subtitle of her book assumes a collective human obligation—*Our Obligations to Other Animals*—rather than thinking about the differences among humans.[36] Nevertheless, by thinking about how values are tethered to *who we are*, she does provide a way to question and criticize the ways in which human norms are invoked to assume that our lives have greater value. In her previous work, Korsgaard had already closed the gap between selves and norms; it's not that there is some neutral substrate of selfhood to which values are added but rather that the formation of the self is made possible by normativity.[37] To be a self is to have values that are definitive. Korsgaard extends a broadly Kantian antifoundationalism, where there is no ground for morality other than the law we give to ourselves; it is this relation to law that produces the self as a moral animal. The self is nothing other than its ongoing formation through decisions, with each decision having no ground other than the ongoing pattern produced through a commitment to being the person one happens to be. Rather than thinking of a consistent self whose being is the ground from which decisions follow, it is the pattern and rhythm of decisions that form a self. One might say, "That is not something I would do," *or* one might imagine that an absence of all patterns for decisions would be the abandonment of any sense of self or personhood. One might think of selfhood and norms as an attachment to being who one is, a sense of maintaining oneself. One might think of this ethically, as Korsgaard invites us to do, or one might think of this attachment to self in formal or cinematic terms. The self or "I" is brought about through the habit of perceptions, with those perceptions being composed through the various media one consumes. Normativity, for Korsgaard, is inescapable given that actions and decisions compose (and are composed by) the life we have given ourselves; we are bound to who we are. This brings us perilously close to the Nietzschean notion that there is no doer behind the deed and that personhood is an effect of what happens.[38] This might be seen ethically as an ongoing formation through principles and reasons for acting, or it might take the structure of an ex post facto narrative effect that emerges from traversing or occupying space: there is action; therefore I am. In the case of postapocalyptic culture, this might be altered to a point of view in which having brought the world to the brink of destruction, this is now the world *we* have. The "we" just is this attachment and follows from a history of violence that must justify itself with the promise of a future.

End of World and "World"

A specific sense of "world" was articulated early in the twentieth century, but the notion that "world" refers to a horizon of sense goes well beyond philosophy. Rather than think of the world and the end of the world as objects, the phenomenological tradition reduced "world" to the horizon of sense from which subject and object unfold. Husserl referred to this reduction as a philosophical method whereby one would not assume any external existence of the world but would attend *only* to what appears.[39] The world would always be a lifeworld (*Lebenswelt*), always unfolding from the lived. What began as a phenomenological method became a theory of the world. It is not that there is a world that subsequently appears; the world *is* its appearing. We are always already in the world, with the concepts of subject and object becoming possible only *after* the world has come into being through appearing.[40] One of the most trenchant criticisms of this tradition was made by Quentin Meillassoux, who argued that tying the world to subjectivity precluded thinking of the very real existence of the world prior to the existence of humans. Meillassoux's own response was to argue that rather than think of *subjectivity* as foundational, it is contingency that is the only (and non-metaphysical) absolute.[41] Rather than the world as a horizon of sense being the transcendental ground of any possible experience, Meillassoux insists that experience is contingent and that anything that is experienced could also not be. It is perfectly possible to imagine the world without humans and perfectly possible to imagine no world at all. Anything that is could also not be. What remains is contingency. This speculative realist gesture returns the absolute to what can be thought. Meillassoux's criticism marks out a clear opposition: either the world is nothing more than that which appears to the subject or we have the courage to think of contingency—no world, no subject, no life. Meillassoux might therefore be the philosopher of the postapocalyptic present par excellence: either one affirms the world as absolute or there is nothing at all. (This is not quite fair, as his focus is on *the world of subjectivity in general*. But that is just the problem. There is something other than the stark choice between the world as appearance for a subject and the thought and speculation of contingency.) Rather than be trapped in the notion that either there is a world that appears to the subject or one must think the absolute of utter contingency, one could think of different ways of thinking outside or beyond the subject. Meillassoux's criticism of correlationism is profound: to reduce the world to what appears is a complete failure of thinking. What would be more significant than thinking about the absolute of contingency that lies outside correlation would be to imagine other ways of exiting the world. One possibility would be to think of both subjectivity and the absolute as but one among many ways of imagining existence.

Within the phenomenological tradition, there was already a tendency toward thinking beyond the world and certainly beyond the subject. Even if, as with Meillassoux, there was a valorization of thinking, the task of thought was to trace its own capacity from what might be thought of as being, life, matter, or force. Following or tracking a path of being creates an attachment. There is not space across which movement takes place nor beings that then move in order to take up space, but a space unfolds from movements that create a field of relative stability. This notion that stable beings and their milieus are the effect of relations among forces might be referred to as a "field metaphysic" in a tradition that runs from Spinoza to the present.[42] In the twentieth century, it was Deleuze's reading of Spinoza, and his mobilization of the work of Gilbert Simondon, that sought to displace the fetishized attachment to world and subjectivity. In doing so he posed a challenge: Would it be possible to forge an immanent philosophy—one that did not explain the unfolding of the world from the lived experience of the subject? This is, indeed, a philosophical question, but its political and aesthetic consequences are significant. If forces and fields unfold from subjects, then it would be possible to think of the decline of subjectivity as the end of the world, and this was indeed a key feature of twentieth-century philosophy and modernism. Rather than refer to a self or subject, Heidegger's use of *Da-sein* ("there-being") marked the ways in which identity is constituted through existing in a distinct place.[43] And while Heidegger opened the thought of existence beyond the notion of the subject for whom there is a world and instead thought of *Da-sein* as the "there" where being comes to appear, he also insisted that there were beings who were poor in world—beings who were nothing more than their range of responses to their milieu.[44] A world is a form of life, but it might also be the case that only some forms of life think of themselves as *worldly*.

The European tradition of phenomenology presupposed and reinforced the idea that to be a self was to harbor a horizon of sense and possibility that was one's own and that one's world was bounded by one's own death. Death marks the finite range of possibilities that delimit and individuate a life; without death, every subject would go through the possibilities of every other. (An animal, supposedly, has no sense of death or ownness, no sense of the horizon of decisions being constitutive of an individuated life.) To know that one dies is to know that one lives *this* life and no other. This also raises the question of forms of life that do not fetishize the horizon of one's own death. To think of oneself as nothing more than a fragment of eternity, and to live *as if* for all time, would be but one way to imagine the end of the world. To think of one's life *sub specie aeternitatis* might render personal, privatized, and individualist lives meaningless, but there are other forms of individuation. End-of-world culture knows only one modality of meaning and world; without the sense of one's own world, there is no world at all.

There might be worlds that do not fetishize the unique horizons of ownness that unfold from highly individuated persons.

Or to make this less abstract, one might ask why postapocalyptic culture imagines the end of urban individualism as the end per se. Why is the end of the bourgeois family and urban affluence imagined as the end of all horizons of sense and value?

When Heidegger claimed that animals were "poor" in world, he made explicit the assumption that proper existence *for us* requires not simply surviving in a space but having a sense of ownness—that one is here in this world that has been marked off from all others. For Heidegger an animal has a space of possibility but is not marked off by the decisive difference of human existence. *Da-sein* is the being that follows from being *there* (the marking out of a space or world). When Heidegger adds to this sense of ownness that no one can die for me, because one's life is a "being-toward-death," he enhances the stakes of ownness to a matter of life and death. It is because I die, and occupy this moment in time and no other, that I cannot exist and live as if all things were possible. My death delimits my existence to *this here*, but that also means that my life—bounded by death—marks itself off from the life and death of others. I cannot act, as Nietzsche's "eternal return" demands, as if eventually I would live through all possibilities; it is my death that makes this expanse of time and action *mine* and not yours. What might it mean, today, to question this attachment to ownness? Such a question is prompted by the possible end of the world. If we seek to save the world, whose world will survive, and what of the world cannot be saved?

2

Technologies of the Self

What Heidegger never thought through was the extent to which ownness, being there, and being toward death were dependent on inscriptive technologies—not merely the capacity to say "I" but the more complex narrative strategies that mark out a time and place as "mine" or "ours." Such technologies need not be human and might be discerned in many different ways in which lives are formed. Gilles Deleuze and Félix Guattari described individuation as the articulation of a refrain. Birdsong, the assemblage of nests, webs, burrows, or the dancing movements of migration are, for Deleuze and Guattari, forms of expression that precede and make possible the distinctions of identity.[1] The specifically humanist sense of ownness as bound up with nothing more than the trajectory of one's life delimited by death is made possible by quite specific narrative forms and techniques of point of view. In *Reading for the Plot* Peter Brooks compares the narrative arc typical of the novel to Freud's death drive—an initial disturbance finds resolution and closure but does so in its own way.[2] All stories begin with a desire for the end, but the end must be a coherent fulfilment of an initial lack. With the modern Western novel, the trajectory and resolution become increasingly private.

In his history of ethics, the neo-Aristotelian philosopher

Alasdair MacIntyre argues that selves would increasingly become the ground from which rights and morality would be constructed rather than—as they had been for Homer, Aristotle, Jane Austen, and Benjamin Franklin—the outcome of social and political relations grounded on practices. The literary history that leads into the modern novel moves increasingly inward, to the point that MacIntyre diagnoses the present as one in which selves are distinct from the stability of character and are pure capacities for decision; one decides as one feels:

> The specifically modern self, the self that I have called emotivist, finds no limits set to that on which it may pass judgment for such limits could only derive from rational criteria for evaluation, and, as we have seen, the emotivist self lacks any such criteria. Everything may be criticized from whatever standpoint the self has adopted including the self's choice of standpoint to adopt. It is in this capacity of the self to evade any necessary identification with any particular contingent state of affairs that some modern philosophers, both analytical and existentialist, have seen the essence of moral agency. To be a moral agent is, on this view, precisely to be able to stand back from any and every situation in which one is involved, from any and every characteristic that one may possess, and to pass judgment on it from a purely universal and abstract point of view that is totally detached from all social particularity. Anyone and everyone can thus be a moral agent, since it is in the self and not in social roles or practices that moral agency has to be located.[3]

Selves are, for MacIntyre, the effect of social relations and not foundations that precede relationality. MacIntyre's criticism of the self as a world of its own goes some way toward destroying a humanism that begins with a normative and pure conception of the subject, but it replaces that subjective ground with the normatively human polity. MacIntyre argues for a social conception of the self, but the socius is also the outcome of relations. The *political* sense of the socius—that we are beings formed through human relations—differs from more cosmic understandings where we would be formed through relations to the elements, to nonhuman animals, and to lakes, rivers, mountains, and the sun.

How do polities come into being? How are worlds composed, and why do philosophers of sympathy (such as Nussbaum) or sociality (such as MacIntyre) not think about forms of narrative that exist outside the humanist tradition? One answer is that this is simply not their project. Yet it is worth questioning the limits of such philosophical attachments to the novel. If the private world of the novel—with its reflective ease of dialogue made possible by spaces of leisure—comes under global and planetary pressure, then it makes sense to ask about the literary formation of other worlds. If we are components of a lifeworld, what brings a lifeworld into being? It is interesting and telling that neo-Aristotelian philosophers who rely heavily on literature and the sense of life as narrative tend to halt their interest in the novel with modernism. Once writing becomes a force in its own right and once self *and world* are presented as the outcome of inscriptive technologies, neo-Aristotelians lose interest. MacIntyre declares Jane Austen to be "the last great effective imaginative voice of the tradition of thought about, and practice of, the virtues which I have tried to identify."[4] Things start to fall apart, for MacIntrye, after Henry James; James was able to diagnose a world in which morality had come to be nothing more than a game, contrasted with a world in which ethics still had a sense of the social whole.[5] It is with modernism that point of view becomes increasingly cinematic; a character is not the exploration of a possible ethics but the effect of the patterns and rhythms of a place. James Joyce's *Dubliners* depicts the city as a series of habits, including linguistic habits but also—as will happen to a greater extent in *Ulysses*—the habits of taste and smell. The self is the sights, sounds, smells, and textures it encounters. It is as though a character is the effect of its perceptions. High-modernist texts, such as *Ulysses* or Virginia Woolf's *The Waves*, chart the fall of perceptions onto the plane of consciousness, as though the brain were a screen.[6] For the most part, twentieth-century and twenty-first-century fiction have taken the form of mapping a character's perceptions; identity is the effect of what happens. Bret Easton Ellis's *American Psycho* is about a serial killer; but rather than capture his thoughts and feelings, the text is largely made up of listing the products he consumes. The opening paragraph begins with a scrawled sign, with the novel's central character emerging from the sounds and sensations he consumes:

> ABANDON ALL HOPE YE WHO ENTER HERE is scrawled in blood red lettering on the side of the Chemical Bank near the corner of Eleventh and First and is in print large enough to be seen from the backseat of the cab as it lurches forward in the traffic leaving Wall Street and just as Timothy Price notices the words a bus pulls up, the advertisement for *Les Misérables* on its side blocking his view, but Price who is with Pierce & Pierce and twenty-six doesn't seem to care because he tells the driver he will give him five dollars to turn up the radio, "Be My Baby" on WYNN, and the driver, black, not American, does so.[7]

If a dominant strand in Anglo-American fiction depicts selves as the effect of perceptions, this still allows for the possibility that the self is something like a blank slate that is then imprinted by experiences. It is one thing to accept that selves are the effects of experience, but quite another—and far more interesting— possibility is that selves as individual subjects are the effects of experiences synthesized by visual technologies. The evolution of the reading eye is tied to an archive of external memory technologies, from cave painting to cinema and smartphones. Humanity is the effect of technologies of perception and stored memory. Such technologies include cityscapes that channel perceptions and capture attention, as well as novels and films that produce sympathy and attachment.

Bernard Stiegler has argued for an "arche-cinema" in which what comes to be known as "the human" is the effect of perceiving images that store the experiences and desires of the past.[8] Stiegler's sense of inscriptive and memory-storing technologies is broad; the archive is not just the history of visual and literary art but includes the day-to-day objects that allow habits and comportments to be passed on. What is distinct about the history of inscriptive technologies is the production of individuation and the marking of time. To perceive an animal and to read its tracks for the purposes of hunting is one thing; but to see a picture of an animal painted on a cave is to be directed to someone else's perception and desire. The eye becomes a reading rather than tracking eye, oriented to *someone* whose world is also (at least in part) one's own. The world in its rich phenomenological sense as a horizon of possibilities emerges from the long history of perceptual technologies; archives are world formative. Various forms of inscription work against entropy; they give desire a form and temporality that creates more complex relations, desires, and distinctions among individuals. The human is essentially cinematic, brought into being by way of the collective consumption and production of stored images, and "negentropic"—formed through technologies that enable complexity and desire to be expanded and intensified across time. For Stiegler, arche-cinema is a way of thinking about the genesis and possibility of the human, beings who are made possible by technologies that take desire toward a formation of spirit. This, for Stiegler, is the problem of saving the world—the world is formed through technologies that allow desire to be preserved and intensified across time. Save the archive; save the world. It is only through the things we care about that we exist at all.

The eye of the camera is, for the time of the film, who we are. And as long as we exist, the camera keeps rolling; or as long as the camera keeps rolling, there is a "we" of the film.[9] It is not that there is a subject who perceives, nor even a "we" that develops its ways of seeing, but rather that the "we" is the effect of perceptions. Holding on to who we are requires the ongoing care for the archive. Postapocalyptic cinema makes this all too apparent, focused as it is on both the spectacle of the world falling apart and the curation of the things that memorialize who we are. The human is a perceptual-archival assemblage that increasingly bears within itself the potential for its own end. Stiegler has referred to this condition (following Derrida) as the *pharmakon*; the external stored memories of the archive yield the complexity of desire and time that enable the distinction of the human. But if those technologies take on an industrial scale that is detached from the capacities of any individual body, then we arrive at the proletarianization of sensibility.[10] Our desires are not only not our own (ownness being an effect of desiring composition) but can also be simplified into the mere repetition of immediate consumption. The cinema and arche-cinema that once extended desire beyond the mere immediacy of the drive might become nothing more than the production of stereotypes, simply repeating the already given. We would then be increasingly disinvested from the images that compose us, no longer able to care for or cultivate their existence. Stiegler's concern for maintaining the human is neither uncritical nor nostalgic; his history of inscriptive technologies acknowledges both an immanent risk of the inhuman within the human and the brutal conditions of labor that enable the leisure of thinking to be distinguished from the mere work of existing.

> There is a *catastrophe*, in terms of the political decadence of capitalist democracies, a catastrophe in the sense that a new industrial model, and *by the same token a cultural, and therefore political, model*, must be conceived and implemented, and this must take place at a continental level—that of Europe—as an entirely new notion of capitalism-become-cultural, on a worldwide scale. *Within the current capitalism typical of control societies, the function of culture has been reduced to socializing production by standardizing consumer behaviour, culture thereby becoming the agent par excellence of this control.* Now, as I have said elsewhere, and as I will return to in what follows, this control is an exploitation of libidinal energy that *exhausts* this energy, and it is in this way that the industrial model emerging from twentieth-century modernity reaches its limit, particularly in Europe and principally in wealthy Europe.
>
> Encountering this limit, which constitutes an immense danger, is also a chance: it is the chance to invent, *at the moment when the mutation of the technical system makes possible new arrangements*, another social model, which could foreshadow a new stage of becoming of the industrial democracies of the entire world.[11]

Stiegler's work resonates with postapocalyptic culture's insistence that the human, for all its violence and toxicity, is nevertheless that which must be both saved and destroyed for the sake of the future. What we happen to have been must be cast off to find who we properly are. If postapocalyptic cinema unthinkingly and repeatedly admits the harms of the past while affirming the inevitable triumph of the future, Stiegler is far more aware of the risks of the human and its capacity to be nothing more than the passive and entropic consumer of images of its own end. Stiegler's orientation toward the future is not at all concerned with saving humanity as it is. Rather, his attention is directed to the negentropic capacities of cultural technologies. The forces that make culture possible—stored memories—also threaten culture with dissolution. How might we *care* about this possibility rather than allowing for the full takeover of late capitalism? How do we take hold of who we have become? There is, however, another way to think about the cinematic toxicity of the human. Like Stiegler, Deleuze and Guattari are indebted to Simondon and Andre Leroi-Gourhan and the theories of transindividuation and technological evolution that would enable the human to be an effect of relations that bring individuated beings into distinction. Once humanity and the world of humanism is understood to be an effect of relations, one might think about the future as a negotiation of those relations to save a fragile and inessential humanity, *or* one might start to think about an affirmative sense of the end of the world. To destroy the world might allow for the perception of other modes of existence not premised on the self-attachments of an increasingly private subject.

One of the less noted debts of Deleuze and Guattari's work is the inspiration they take from Franz Fanon and an accompanying *anti*oedipal sense that the human is but *one* way in which one might think of existence and one that ought to be placed within a history of colonization and racialization. The subject for whom the world is a structure of sense beyond which lies the dark night of chaos is the outcome of a history in which complex social machines are contracted until we arrive at the private individual whose desires have been rendered personal and familial. If we are the effect of a history of evolving perceptions that can be mapped in relation to technologies, it would be both possible *and desirable* to think of potentialities beyond the human, because desire itself transcends and precedes the human. What makes Fanon's work so important today becomes evident when reading Deleuze and Guattari's debt to Fanon. It may make sense to experience one's desire as being at odds with one's world; it might also be necessary—to quote Fanon quoting Aimé Césaire—to demand the end of the world:

> we sing of poisonous flowers
> bursting in meadows of fury;
> skies of love struck by clots of blood;
> epileptic mornings; the white
> burning of abyssal sands, the sinking of wrecked ships in
>   the middle of nights rent by
> the smell of wild beasts.
> What can I do?
> I must begin.
> Begin what?
> The only thing in the world that's worth beginning:
> The End of the World, no less.[12]

In the broad movement of Afropessimism that has taken up the thought of Fanon, there are two senses in which the end of the world might be imagined. The first would be the end of this world—capitalism and its inherent anti-Blackness—while the second would be the end of the valorization of human existence as being rich in world. What might it mean to think of world-lessness, or being poor in world, as an alternative to saving the world? In many ways postapocalyptic culture hints at an answer, albeit negatively. The end of the world would amount to stateless existence, a loss of the global technologies and industries that create a single humanity, and an abandonment of hyperconsumption and its attendant violence. The end of the world would be the end of the cinematic aesthetic that defines subjectivity as a capacity to view the world as if it were one's own horizon of sense, unfolding from the syntheses and decisions of the individual.

Time, Cinema, and World

What Deleuze and Guattari refer to as "becoming-imperceptible" is preceded by what they refer to as "becoming-animal" and "becoming-woman."[13] These terms occur in *A Thousand Plateaus*, but it is worth bearing in mind that in Deleuze's corpus "becoming" is intertwined with the possibility of cinema *and* with the end of the world. For Deleuze, the actual occurrence of cinema in the twentieth century allows us to rethink the history of the concept of time. Here Deleuze partly draws upon Henri Bergson's criticism of the everyday understanding of time, where we imagine time as a linking together of still moments, in the way that cinema links frames to produce the illusion of movement. For Deleuze, Bergson's criticism of cinematic time offers a path toward thinking about time in its pure state, which would be a time *not* grounded in the human body. Where Bergson laments the cinematic notion of time as a series of pieced-together stills, Deleuze argues that images released from the sensory motor apparatus of the human body enable a thought of time beyond the point of view of the subject. Rather, it is the flow of images that creates points of view, or individuated beings. The capacity for cinema to cut and paste images of movement produces perceptions not grounded in a human point of view. In this respect, cinema is bound up with the end of the world, capable of releasing perceptions from the point of view of the lived.

If, following phenomenology (and the sense of "the world" that is assumed when we worry about the end of the world), the world unfolds from our possibilities for action and if our perceptions are synthesized from the "sensory motor apparatus" of the human body, then images detached from this flow of movement would open up the end of the world. If one thinks of the world as something to be pieced together and synthesized by the mind, then the absence of human existence would be the absence of the world. Without the thinking subject who brings the world's disparate parts into relation, there would be no grand horizon of sense. In this respect there is something cinematic about the Western conception of the human. It is the capacity to synthesize and bring perceptions into some comprehensive whole that brings the world into being. Kant argued that without synthesis there could be no world at all and tied the transcendental subject to the very possibility of the world in its lived sense. For Kant, it is *as if* the world we experience were given to us for the sake of our subjective harmony, *as if* a world not conducive to the sense we make of it cannot really be considered:

> This law of reproduction, however, presupposes that the appearances themselves are actually subject to such a rule, and that in the manifold of their representations an accompaniment or succession takes place according to certain rules; for without that our empirical imagination would never get to do anything suitable to its capacity, and would thus remain hidden in the interior of the mind, like a dead and to us unknown facility. If cinnabar were now red, now black, now light, now heavy, if a human being were now changed into this animal shape, now into that one, if on the longest day the land were covered now with fruits, now with ice and snow, then my empirical imagination would never even get the opportunity to think of heavy cinnabar on the occasion of the representation of the color red; or if a certain word were attributed now to this thing, now to that, or if one and the same thing were sometimes called this, sometimes that, without the governance of a certain rule to which the appearances are already subjected in themselves, then no empirical synthesis of reproduction could take place.[14]

We become and know who we are through the exercise of our capacity for synthesis: "for without that our empirical imagination would never get to do anything suitable to its capacity, and would thus remain hidden in the interior of the mind, like a dead and to us unknown facility." Coherent synthesis—something like a camera that links frames to form movement and a coherent narrative—becomes the condition for the world *and* the subject who brings that world to light. It is this conception of time as akin to a camera piecing still moments together that Bergson will criticize in his attempt to think of time in its pure state, a time before we have managed and edited images into a world *for us*.[15] It is a modified cinematic conception of synthesis that allows Deleuze to think of what he refers to as irrational cuts, or those that could not be lived from an embodied point of view. Rather than still images pieced together, Deleuze looks at the way cinema connects movements. What separates Bergson from Deleuze is their different attachments to the lived. In the early twentieth century, Bergson was part of a broader movement that resisted human mechanization and the reduction of spirit to the inertia of matter; to think of the mind as something that pieces together fragments of the world to produce movement missed the creative flow and spirit of the world. For Deleuze, it was precisely this machinic capacity that would enable philosophy to free itself from the normativity of man and the body that folds perceptions around its own interests and attachments. Cinema displays the capacity for images to be cut from the lived and, in that respect, enables a thought of what lies beyond us. Cinema and the philosophy it made possible enabled, for Deleuze, a way of making thought genuinely cosmic rather than parochial.[16] Deleuze was primarily interested in the *formal* capacities of cinema and the way in which a technology could free perceptions from lived experience. It follows that if cinema has the capacity to release images from attachments, it is also crucial to subject formation.

Most postapocalyptic cinema organizes its images to create

an attachment to the world and to a highly specific figure of humanity. Often this is done with quite explicit modes of framing, so that a cinematic "we" looks upon the rest of the world as either collateral damage, witless spectator, or less fortunate others to be saved. In *Arrival* (Denis Villeneuve, 2016) alien invasion is a global threat but is depicted from the point of view of a mother who—as a linguist—is charged with the capacity of translating alien messages. The cinematic frame in *Arrival* tracks the narrative from the point of view of the team of scientists who are assessing and negotiating the alien presence. The viewer also sees images of the mother's dreams, so that we are both viewing the aliens from the point of view of earthly interrogators and from the interiority of a mother mourning the loss of her child. It turns out that the aliens are seeking to deliver a universal language, but it is only the U.S. linguist who approaches these others with a spirit of translation. Non-U.S. governments regard the extraterrestrials as combatants. The "we" of the film is tied to an America that is open to the universe, while other nations are hostile and combative—incapable of the expansive vision of recognition. The film's narrative marks out an opposition between them and us, at first the aliens and humanity and then the conciliatory and peace-seeking United States of knowledge and understanding versus the China of warcraft. The plot twist occurs when the central character's dreams of her dead daughter are revealed to be messages from the aliens, sent thousands of years ago so that they could be received in the present—via the dreams of the child—in order to save humanity from itself. If eternity could speak, it would do so via the dreams of an American child. Saving the world, in *Arrival*, is once again the redemption of an ideal of America and is enabled by the technology of language, which (in its fantasized mode) creates a single humanity of the present that becomes the vehicle for universal understanding.

3

Save the World

Not only is the avoidance of the end of the world at the heart of common sense, such that all other disasters can be ameliorated by the consolation that "it's not the end of the world," but saving the world becomes structural to postapocalyptic culture and the most highly funded levels of twenty-first-century government and corporate research. The heroic narratives of possible world annihilation, from the alien-invasion epics of 1950s sci-fi to the climate change catastrophes of the twenty-first century, suggest that nothing is more cinematically pleasurable than saving the world from its end. Alongside those fantasies of saving the world from aliens, viruses, zombies, and climate catastrophe are the day-to-day imperatives to recycle, buy sustainable goods, manage one's carbon footprint, and use local suppliers. The notion that we ought to act locally but think globally is grounded in a presupposed "we" and in a shared future. This silent and underlying commonality is explicit in an increasing number of think tanks and research centers that focus on saving who we are. Oxford's Future of Humanity Institute has a distinct idea of what counts as humanity; Future Earth is oriented to sustainability,[1] and Earth Futures at the University of California is premised on the urgency of humanity needing help.[2] The ongoing task of *saving the world* is not a new postapocalyptic concern; it is at the very heart of the concepts of the world and the human. What marks the twenty-first century is the far more explicit threat of climate chaos and the far more explicit and shrill affirmation of a single humanity.

Well before the end of the world became a common fictional and cinematic motif, the West had constituted itself by way of the world-saving concepts of lifeworld and the artworld. In phenomenology the lifeworld, or *Lebenswelt*, is the horizon of sense and meaning that allows the subject to encounter everything in terms of an ongoing retained past and an anticipated future—always assuming that this world for me is also there for others with their own meanings. When Heidegger claimed that animals were "poor in world," it was this sense of individuated lifeworld that he was drawing upon; apart from paying less attention to the complexity of animal worlds than he might have done,[3] Heidegger failed to question richer senses of techne, cosmos, and nature that might have gone beyond a world that unfolds from a sense of ownness. A lot depends on how one defines and delimits techne and whether one might grant a historical and spatial complexity to non-Western forms of cosmology. While some histories of Indigenous peoples have insisted on the technological sophistication of the cultures that were displaced by Western invasion,[4] it is also necessary to question the privilege attached to technological maturity.[5] This would not only expand the range of human normativity and excellence beyond societies with industrialized agriculture but also open the sense of what worlds might be possible.[6] Postapocalyptic images of the end of the world and white colonizer's images of the "New World" are startlingly similar. Nomadic wandering, no obvious signs of hyperconsumption, no industries of privacy that fold individuals around information technologies appeared as terra nullius. The path of humanity has been tied to a path of economic growth and progress, while those peoples whose worlds did not rely on the planetary transformations definitive of the Anthropocene were deemed to be poor in world. What comes to be forged as the human is haunted by this background of worldlessness. In a tradition that goes back at least as far as Kant, the notion of a necessary horizon of sense that ties any experience of the world to the experience of presupposed others is inextricably bound up with a human project of saving the world and of increasingly drawing attention to the single history and horizon of sense that will include, recognize, comprehend, and survey all other worlds.

The implicit saving of the world that is at the heart of the transcendental humanist project of recognition is particularly evident in the artworld, with the great galleries of Western modernity providing a panorama of all the worlds that give themselves forth in a series of expressive art objects—masks, vases, urns, armor, jewelry, or weapons can be taken from their world and viewed as fragments of a single globe that varies through time and can be saved and stored in the final stages of the West. Emily St. John Mantel's 2014 novel *Station Eleven* follows dispersed humans who hold on to memories of Shake-speare and make their way across a postapocalyptic earth to a "museum of humanity."[7] *Station Eleven* thematizes the world as one of attachments, a world that recognizes itself only insofar as it remembers and gathers itself, holding on to Shakespeare, while also assembling itself for the memory of humanity to come. In postapocalyptic cinema, it is often the possession of the last few memorial objects that hold subjects together. In *Oblivion* (Joseph Kosinski, 2013) a drone repairman left on Earth to extract the last dregs of resources holds on to a few remaining items in order to be something more than a colonized subject. A shelf of books, sunglasses, a baseball, baseball cap, and a recording of late 1960s British Rock allow the nostalgia within the film to be a nostalgia for us, as though we could see the things of our world becoming souvenirs of who we once were. Such things of the present and recent past placed in a future where they have become fragments of a lost world allow our world to appear as wistfully valuable for future humans. We appear to be less inclined to imagine the future looking back on us with resentment, amazed that there was once a time without survival lotteries and utter scarcity.[8]

There are minor hints of accusation that have been articulated in the postapocalyptic canon, but they are inevitably accompanied with the sense that at the heart of destruction there was a shining spirit of humanism whose loss can only be tragic. *Planet of the Apes* (Franklin Schaffner, 1968) sees a ruined Statue of Liberty washed up on the shores of a future in which humans are now the enslaved servants of apes. Even though the central character, Taylor, reacts to this wreckage by damning a past humanity—"You finally really did it, you maniacs, you blew it up, ah damn you"—the horror of the film lies in humanity's enslavement by some species that deems itself to be superior. What is being mourned is the loss of humanity's species dominance, a dominance that ought to have prevailed had we not been quite so arrogant. The tragedy is registered in this symbol of freedom—the Statue of Liberty—becoming unrecognizable, appearing as so much detritus. The end of the world is the collapse of the archive of things that has composed who we are. Postapocalyptic landscapes are littered with lost objects. In *I Am Legend* Neville's last days in New York are spent watching the library of DVDs he is able to gather from a derelict store. There is a survival imperative in the gathering of lost things; postapocalyptic landscapes are postproduction landscapes, where finding the last vestiges of industry enables life to continue. The only foods left in McCarthy's *The Road* (apart from cannibalism) are the leftover tins in abandoned houses. Capitalism after the end of the world takes on a statuesque quality; from the books and baseball caps in *Oblivion* to the deserted mall in Ling Ma's novel *Severance*, the things that remain are the last vestiges of who we are. *Severance* hints at an exit from this attachment—the mall of things that will be the last vestige of humanity becomes a prison from which the central character, pregnant, chooses to escape. In doing so, the standard postapocalyptic axiology is destroyed. If it is generally assumed that a world without hyperconsumption is no world at all, *Severance* chooses to exit the mall that could be the last hope for humanity. Better to face the world, pregnant and alone, than to be held within the suffocation of capitalism's last things.

The question ought not to be how to save the world but rather how to imagine life after the world of hyperconsumption. Despite the incapacity to imagine the end of capitalism as anything other than the end of the world, the hyperconsumption that constitutes the world has also often been marked as already destructive of the world. Often a yearning for a world without things is a colonizing nostalgia that valorizes a humanity purified of hyperconsumption at the same time as it will define humanity narrowly as beings who are tragically cut off from the paradise of statelessness. Not only was the "New World" conveniently regarded as unoccupied because of the absence of things; that same poorness in world was romanticized as a figure of our lost past. The technology that constitutes progress and humanity is marked off from a necessarily lost innocence that is also, despite its desirability, not properly human. Rousseau related the weakening of civilization directly to the acquisition of things, and yet such things also marked the distance from "savagery." The becoming-world of the world amounts to a loss of self:

> Since the savage man's body is the only instrument he knows, he employs it for a variety of purposes that, for lack of practice, ours are incapable of serving. And our industry deprives us

of the force and agility that necessity obliges him to acquire. If he had had an axe, would his wrists break such strong branches? If he had had a sling, would he throw a stone with so much force? If he had had a ladder, would he climb a tree so nimbly? If he had had a horse, would he run so fast? Give a civilized man time to gather all his machines around him, and undoubtedly he will easily overcome a savage man. But if you want to see an even more unequal fight, pit them against each other naked and disarmed, and you will soon realize the advantage of constantly having all of one's forces at one's disposal, of always being ready for any event, and of always carrying one's entire self, as it were, with one.[9]

One might also say—and this is a sense I want to explore in this chapter—that well before we arrived at the current crisis of the Anthropocene, there was already a sense of the end of the world at the very heart of what is defined as human.

What Is the World?

The *world* is neither the planet nor the ecosystem nor the global populace but the comportment of human recognition that underpins the Anthropocene's sense of a single historical humanity and the humanist sense of one species that expresses and recognizes itself through various expressions of cultural difference. The world is a horizon of recognition; the *end* of the world is not the end of the planet or of life but the end of the global humanity who cannot contemplate any mode of existence other than that of universal recognition. Without the mass media technologies that beam in images of the globe, we become poor in world. In a quite narrow sense, one might think of all the ways in which the depiction of the end of capitalism—humans wandering nomadically, no longer tethered to global media—is seen as tantamount to the end of the world. In this respect, the motif of the end of the world is inextricably bound up with the utter intolerability of thinking the end of *us*. The only world we can imagine is *the* world that has concerned itself with world saving (always at the expense of ending other worlds precisely by saving them: colonization will always save others from their own ends). Where films such as *Black Panther* or *Avatar* will repeat the colonizing notion that even utopian other worlds should be saved for the sake of saving *us*, the world-saving imperative goes well beyond postapocalyptic cinema in its narrow sense and structures the Manichean narratives of most blockbuster cinema. Whether it is the James Bond franchise's capacity to imagine various evil others (the Russians, the Chinese, the Koreans), depending on the geopolitical landscape of the day, or the disaster-movie genre of any number of threats to *us*, the drama of saving the world intensifies the value of who we are, versus *them*.

Mission Impossible: Fallout (Christopher McQuarrie, 2018) is not explicitly concerned with the end of the world, and unlike much twenty-first-century genre cinema it does not assume the backdrop of climate change and resource depletion. It nevertheless harbors the common assumption that the end of life as we know it amounts to the end of *the world*. Disaster epics, spy fiction, alien-invasion films, or zombie epics parse the narrative drama of good versus evil as the triumph of *us* over *them*, allowing the final stages of vanquishing the other to appear as the triumph of light over dark. In *Mission Impossible: Fallout* the tragic dichotomy between the properly human and the threat of dissolution is located within the hero himself. Ethan Hunt's personality is an allegory of modern ethics. Nothing is more sacred than the life and soul of the individual, and yet the vast complexity of the world constantly threatens to deface that very singularity. The film is premised on this central psychological conflict played out in Ethan's heart. Who would you kill and what would you do to save the world? On the one hand, there is a heroic imperative to save the world, *and yet* one must do so while recognizing the sacredness of every single life. It is this narrative conundrum—the elevation of the sacred individual *despite the loss of life in general*—that once again generates the conclusion that this world of liberal individualism must not end. To lose what we have, to lose the world as it is, would be an unthinkable catastrophe, and no consideration of the losses and violence demanded by this world can justify a loss of what is before me here and now. Not only is *Mission Impossible: Fallout* subtended by the usual catastrophic ideology that privileges the redemption of single characters over the world as such; it also intensifies the modern aesthetic comportment, where the individuals who are valued are those subjects who set themselves apart from the world, capable of elevating themselves above the mass of the globe and life to be fully human. Torn between saving those who are closest to him and saving the world, Ethan is presented as a tragic figure—a noble soul whose ethical beauty has no place in a world of global and corporate ruthlessness. In the end, *Mission Impossible* allows Ethan to save the world while also remaining true to his individual attachments; as with *Interstellar* and *The Adjustment Bureau*, the human freedom and world-conquering spirit that may have led to global catastrophe are challenged only to reemerge in their world-saving rather than world-preserving form.

The sanctity of the individual life is not, and never has been, the sanctity of *any* individual life but the valorization of a specific mode of individualism—the self who is not simply a part of the world but, as Kant would argue, who sees *himself* and every other self as a rational member of the kingdom of ends. The world is there as an occasion for rational elevation; our capacity to give form to the world also enables us to imagine ourselves as free from the mere world. We are beings for whom the apparent order of the world exists. Kant describes this comportment to the world as the end of creation:

> Why do these creatures exist? If one answers: For the animal kingdom, which is nourished by it so that it is able to spread itself over the earth in so many genera, then the question arises again: Why do these herbivorous animals exist? Perhaps the answer would be: For the carnivores, which can only be nourished by what lives. But in the end the question is: For what are these, together with all the proceeding natural kingdoms, good? For the human being, for the diverse uses which his understanding teaches him to make of all these creatures; and he is the ultimate end of the creation here on earth, because he is the only being on earth who forms a concept of ends for himself and who by means of his reason can make a system of ends out of an aggregate of purposively formed things.[10]

The point of view of the modern subject is, then, *Anthroposcenic* rather than anthropocentric. The anthroposcenic aesthetic assumes that a varied, complex, volatile, fragile, and incalculable living system can be viewed, if not mastered, by a humanity that is now unified not by an underlying essence but by a comportment to the future. The more fragile and at risk humanity as a whole becomes, the more it seeks to save and preserve itself. A common feature of postapocalyptic culture is the aesthetic fragment—a volume of Shakespeare, the Bible, the Statue of Liberty, a vinyl record, a child's toy—which can only have sense if someone maintains a memory of their original significance. Less sentimental discourses such as the remit of Future Earth are concerned with transformation, but transformation is ultimately for the sake of sustaining who we are. Like the narrative point of view of the Anthropocene, dispersed innovators and cultures are drawn together so that *we must survive*:

At Future Earth, we are convinced that the only way to accelerate transformations to a more sustainable and equitable planet is for the world to draw on its collective knowledge.

That is why we build on our global network of thousands of researchers to spark and guide scientific inquiry on the planet's land, air and water—and the people and biodiversity that depend on them for their survival. We also recognise that the research community on its own cannot adequately address these challenges. That is why we also collaborate with innovators in policy, business and civil society to generate research that meets society's needs.[11]

Let's set aside the fact that the valorization of the liberal subject—the self of the "we" who gathers and transforms the varied world—has always been the individual elevated by a limited and normative conception of reason and *never* the disindividuated bodies from those portions of the globe who orient themselves toward other conceptions of life. Despite gathering humanity as a species, the Anthropocene has nevertheless intensified a modern form of hyperindividualism, both in the demand that we sustain who we are and in the rhetorical point of view that surveys the whole of time from a situation of appreciation and aesthetic discernment. This not only is true of the heroism of disaster movies but also marks many strands of theory and philosophy.

Stiegler, writing about the Neganthropocene, sees disindividuation as the true catastrophe of the twenty-first century, with climate change being the most evident symptom. We are threatened, he argues, with having *no future* precisely because our evolution as archival beings—from the cave paintings of Lascaux to the art of Marcel Duchamp—has required us to relate to the art object spiritually, imagining the object as signed by a master of the past whose mystique we collectively yearn to relive.[12] For

Stiegler, there is no future without this constitutively human mode of individuation. He accompanies his own yearning for a future with a recognition that the "anthropos" threatened with an end is essentially bound up with a drive to dissolution that it constantly battles.[13] Other less reflective future panics simply assert that it is because the world is threatened with an end that all must be done to save *the* future, where futurity is anything but open. Nearly all our end-of-world narratives are ultimately end-of-liberal-individualism narratives, with the loss of the world providing a backdrop for the heroic elevation and salvation of the man of reason. The humanity that seeks to save and preserve itself is the humanity of global plunder, the being who can gather the world's resources and make them his own.

If common sense and postapocalyptic culture demand that one must save the world as it is, regardless of the losses incurred, then this attachment to the reasoning self of modern liberalism is expressed with even more intensity in the remit of Oxford University's Future of Humanity Institute and its focus on avoiding existential catastrophe, despite what our folkish and sentimental attachments might prompt us to value. In a telling argument, the institute's director, Nick Bostrom, draws on Derek Parfit's philosophy regarding the value of reason and persons. We tend to direct our emotional energies at the massive losses of life that occur with events such as pandemics and genocide, but these—for all their acknowledged horror—ought to be considered from a more rational and global perspective. The real loss that ought to concern us is the loss of rational personhood. Commenting on a graph of world population growth, Bostrom notes, "Calamities such as the Spanish [*sic*] flu pandemic, the two world wars, and the Holocaust scarcely register. (If one stares hard at the graph, one can perhaps just barely make out a slight temporary reduction in the rate of growth of the world population during these events.)"[14] What matters, or ought to matter, is not life as such, not how much suffering or joy there is in the world, but the presence or absence of intellect: "To calculate the loss associated with an existential catastrophe, we must consider how much value would come to exist in its absence. It turns out that the ultimate potential for Earth-originating intelligent life is literally astronomical."[15] This astronomical loss has to do with the fact that if humanity as it is were wiped out today, there would be a loss of not only intelligent life as it is but also intelligent life in terms of its journey toward ever greater forms of complexity and maturity. In short, if we try to avoid events like the Holocaust, then we only save lives; if we do all we can to preserve and develop intelligence, then our efforts are far more worthy, because for Bostrom there is a qualitative difference between millions of lives and the potential for intelligent life: "Even if we use the most conservative of these estimates, which entirely ignores the possibility of space colonization and software minds, we find that the expected loss of an existential catastrophe is greater than the value of 10^{16} human lives. This implies that the expected value of reducing existential risk by a mere one millionth of one percentage point is at least a hundred times the value of a million human lives."[16]

I will leave aside the species arrogance of these calculations and instead focus on the racism that structures the very posing of the problem. How does one manage to divide quantities of lives from a single feature of life—such as the form of intelligence that could be preserved in "software minds"? One simply has to ignore those forms of life that would place more worth and existential value on events of dwelling, moving, or communing with one's nonkin and instead privilege *beyond measure* what Bostrom defines as definitive of humanity—technological maturity. One also has to close the question of what counts as technology, assuming what Viveiros de Castro refers to as "monotechnologism."[17] Here is Bostrom's definition of humanity: "By 'humanity' we here mean Earth-originating intelligent life and by 'technological maturity' we mean the attainment of capabilities affording a level of economic productivity and control over nature close to the maximum that could feasibly be achieved."[18] This definition might appear to be formal to the point of avoiding any form of racism and even speciesism; after all, Bostrom will admit the value of software minds and entertain the possibility that the species might be wiped out while allowing "a new intelligent species" to evolve. But to define humanity by economic productivity and control over nature assumes that the values enjoyed by modern, Western, liberal humans count as intelligence per se and as the only values that would constitute a future: "What makes existential catastrophes especially bad is not that they would show up robustly on a plot like the one in [a graph of world population growth], causing a precipitous drop in world population or average quality of life. Instead, their significance lies primarily in the fact that they would destroy the future."[19] *The future* is the maximization of the single feature of this world—intelligence—that ought to outweigh all other considerations regarding life.

Far from this type of calculation being an elitist assumption of a funded research institution, it is part of a broader inability to imagine the end of this world, or the end of a peculiarity—human technological maturity defined in one highly narrow manner. In this respect, the often cited claim that it is easier to imagine the end of the world than the end of capitalism is especially symptomatic of the ways in which the world as it happens to be has come to stand for the only possible world.[20] It would be more accurate to say that the end of capitalism is imagined all too frequently and always appears as the end of the world. The notion that it is easy to imagine the end of the world might be prompted by the twenty-first century's boom industry of postapocalyptic cinema, but nearly every one of those end-of-world epics is in fact the end of *this* world and the end of capitalism. Two films that I have already mentioned—*Black Panther* and *Mission Impossible*—are not explicitly end-of-the-world films, but they both presuppose that saving this world amounts to saving a form of humanity bound up with technological expansion and a specifically modern Western individualism that can only value life to the extent that it intensifies and purifies who we already are. In this respect, we cannot imagine the end of the world; this incapacity defines who we are. All we happen to imagine are various anodyne erasures of capitalism—from the utopia of Wakanda, which ultimately sets for itself the task of making America great again, to the potential nuclear catastrophe averted in *Mission Impossible*, where one man's noble commitment to roguish individualism is enough to thwart the less-than-human force of the deep state.

The way in which the end of the world has been imagined, and continues to be imagined, configures the end of *the world* in a specifically modern sense—not the world as some space within which human life happens to have existed but the world as that which is given time, sense, and futurity through a specific mode of human existence. The Anthropocene, despite appearing at first as an opening to geological time, has ultimately served to intensify a chauvinistic sense of *the world*—the same technologically oriented humanity that saw its own mode of life as so worthy that it conquered the globe and recognized all others as variants of itself now sees itself as having the task of saving the future, but only from within its own imaginative range.

The Anthroposcene

The modern Western and Anthroposcenic notion of the world requires a single self-forming, self-recognizing, and self-inscribing humanity. The self who looks at the world in its rich variety, recognizing humanity in all its cultural and historical richness, is at one and the same time a self for whom there can only be one world—the world that includes all difference as a variation of the same—and a self whose world already encompasses the virtual end of every other possible world. Viveiros de Castro has referred to "mononaturalism" as the anthropologist's assumption of one world that is perceived differently by multiple cultures. What would tear such a humanist pluralism apart would be a multinaturalism, where nature itself had different ways of forming worlds, including cosmologies that have no sense of the human as a single natural kind that might be mapped on to the species.

Without the world as the horizon that allows various expressions of humanity to be included as differing forms of one ever-varying cultural being, there would be neither the modern vogue for the Anthropocene nor the fetish for playing out an end of the world that is really the end of *a* world that imagines itself as the transcendental plane of humanity in general. The two premises of the Anthropocene—that the existence of a species will be discernible as a geological stratum and that this stratification produces the unity of anthropos in general—rely on a formal omniscient narrator. We survey the globe and its history, diagnose the present, and posit a series of possible origins for the perceived change of the state of the earth as a living system; we direct an interpretive eye at various worlds that contributed to, or suffered from, the journey of an anthropos who arrives at the present of self-recognition. When we consider the end of *the* world, it is this world-encompassing omniscient narrator that is threatened with extinction. This is why end-of-world dramas are played out in modern, globally attuned cities blessed with mass media and hyperconsumption. What must be managed and saved is not the species but the capacity that humanity has developed to recognize and survey the whole. This capacity can take the quite simple material form of mass media, such that disaster epics depict the threat to or the destruction of global networks (e.g., Alfonso Curón's 2013 *Gravity*); but it also takes the more elevated and virtual forms of demanding that humanity hold on to its archive, whether that be the Future of Humanity's conception of technological maturity fulfilling itself in software and AI or the impossibility of thinking that this world of amassing stored cultural objects might not be the only world.

The Anthropocene is at once a claim made within the sciences and an event where the scale and point of view of one science generates a normative conception of self and world. It is not surprising that the temporality and comportment of geology emerges at the same time as the study of humanity and the possibility of human sciences. This was one of the central claims of Michel Foucault's *The Order of Things*: once there is something like a plane of life from which humanity emerges, it becomes possible to see human labor and language as expressions of a ground that can be studied and managed.[21] Once the frame of geological time is opened, it becomes possible to see human existence as an event within a broader milieu of life, and it is also possible to interpret human languages, social structures, cultures, and artifacts as responding to a force of life that humans can know only in its effects. The disputes regarding the dating of the Anthropocene are exactly of this type, and they are ultimately biopolitical and managerial.

We know that there has been a geologically significant alteration of the earth as a living system. We then offer a series of overlapping and sometimes conflicting narratives as to how the present came to take the form that it has.[22] Each one of these narratives, with its normative point of view, also harbors an imperative regarding the future. The narrative eye that looks back and identifies capitalism, intensive agriculture, industrialism, colonization, or nuclear energy as the threshold point for the Anthropocene enables the accusing voice to emerge as futurity's promise. One of the most common and obviously justifiable criticisms of the Anthropocene is that it names the human species as the agent of history, rather than a specific and responsible fragment of humanity. It would be more accurate to talk about the Capitolocene, the White Supremocene, or the Plantationocene.[23] One of the virtues of the use of "anthropos" in discourses of the Anthropocene is, however, just this narrative violence—the notion of a single humanity does not occur late in the day, after the advent of geological change, but is essential to the forms of self-narration that justified colonization, empire, and industrialization. "Anthropos" is neither an idea nor an ideal; it is a series of practices, institutions, habits, comportments, and archives that enables a species to configure itself as a planet-altering and world-saving force. The notion of the human sciences, along with the humanities and the Future of Humanity Institute's research, necessarily harbors a normative conception of the human.[24] In this respect, the Anthropocene is a quite accurate name, not only because geological change has been precipitated by the industries and disciplines of humanity in general but also because the ways in which the Anthropocene has been narrated produce an inescapable humanity to come. This can take the form of Dipesh Chakrabarty's "negative universal history," where the differences of the past are subsumed by a present and future in which we are all implicated. However diverse and multiple history may have been, there is now a "we" confronted with the same risk of a devastating future.[25] The assumption of a single humanity of the future can take the form of the Future of Humanity Institute's conception of humanity as essentially a form of technologically maturing intelligence. It can also take the form of a fetishized relation to cultural difference, where one gazes on the world with an anthropological overview, enjoying humanity in all its rich difference, while the anthropologist's point of view enables translation back into a single sense of "the human." It can take the form of any number of end-of-world sagas where all human life is at risk but where the redemption narrative takes place within New York or Los Angeles. This is what ties the genre of postapocalyptic cinema with many narratives of Anthropocene redemption where *we* save *the* world and secure *our* future. Even though the concern is supposedly for humanity as a whole, united as it is by existential threats, the point of view of narration is concerned to save just that fragment of humanity capable of surveying the whole, appreciating difference, and then demanding a future precisely on the basis that humanity is not reducible to its actual destructive history but can, will, and must reinvent itself into the future.

Fragility and the Politics of Extinction

"I recognize the threat to humanity; therefore I must continue to be." This comportment to the world requires and generates fragility at the same time as it produces an ongoing reaction formation against fragility. In order to secure the forms of modern, global, affluent, and world-purveying liberal freedom that enabled a stable and world-entitled humanity, fragility had to be outsourced. A stable Europe, which could appear to writers such as Kant *as if* it were in accord with the demands of reason, morality, and the pleasures of form, was made possible by colonization, slavery, and the forms of technology that generated vast amounts of waste and cheap labor. The ongoing creation of zones of fragility that allowed the West to secure and enjoy centuries of a harmonious and stabilized climate not only enabled a sense of the properly human as future-oriented, always imagining itself as expanding its freedom and range to those not so blessed with the rights of man; it also allowed humanity proper and its world to be identified with a highly unique form of stability. When that stabilized world comes under threat and when what calls itself humanity starts to experience the forms of fragility that it once imposed on the rest of the world, the imperative to save the world becomes ever more parochial. To lose this privileged portion of humanity would be the end of the world.

In Ridley Scott and Cormac McCarthy's *The Counselor* of 2013—a film that does not at first appear to be about extinction—an early scene depicts the leopard-print-wearing Cameron Diaz watching two wild animals tear each other to shreds. Such a scene would appear to be definitively depoliticizing. Nature is red in tooth and claw, and the thin veneer of civilization is a lie. Violence is natural. This might seem to be a unifying thread in McCarthy's work, where the polity and civility occlude a default state of violence. *The Counselor* (like McCarthy's novel *The Road*) might be read as a countertext to all the humanizing and affirmative postapocalyptic epics that save the world and might seem to be positing a "natural" metaphysical violence rather than any political diagnosis. Both *The Road* and *The Counselor* appear to be confronting the simple brutality of life; and in so doing, McCarthy appears to be presenting a reactionary counterpolitics. What *should* be considered as historical and the outcome of relations among humans is presented as if it were the default position of nature. Where *The Road* presents the father and son as fragile, with ethical light traversing a terrain of violence and cannibalism, *The Counselor*'s depiction of the human enjoyment of animal violence presents a stark opposition between the brutish state of nature and the detachment of a civilized human observer. An apolitical, existential, or perhaps even humanist reading of *The Counselor* would regard this opening scene as a reminder that if one strips away the fragile fabric of civility, one arrives at the sheer horror and shudder of existence; only with the social bonds and fabric of political relations are we distanced from mere life. A *political* reading might see the film's presentation of base animality *and* its cinematic enjoyment as the outcome of an ongoing Western mythography that puts violence, brutishness, and immediacy at the heart of a non-Western nature, elevating the Western viewer above mere life; this binary is, in turn, generated by a long history of geopolitical contracts and the projection of savagery onto the non-West. *The Counselor* would be a classic example of myth or ideology. Roland Barthes defined myth as frozen history;[26] what is produced among humans and by way of a history of exchange and conflict is simply presented as the way things are.

McCarthy's entire corpus, like so much Western literature, seems poised between positing a default violence of nature that is always one bad drug deal away (and just across the border in Mexico) and a more critical analysis of the ways in which this supposed non-Western state of "nature" is produced by the West itself, not only in its political practices but also in its self-conception. *The Counselor*'s early scene of animal violence is viewed from a position of leisured ease and is less about violence *itself* than the libidinal investment in violence. The very notion of *violence itself* is cinematic, made possible by taking up a position in relation to what is produced as the supposed immediacy of the world. Practices of depicting the historical and political chaos of the world as natural are crucial to the ongoing production of a border between a civilized "us" and a prepolitical "them." Barthes, heavily influenced by Marxism in his account of myth, suggested that unfreezing myth would entail confronting the symbolic production of nature. Nature is always within human history, and any depiction of a state of nature is really a depiction of the ways in which we imagine what exists beyond our own political comfort zone. Depictions of a noble savage, a primitive and violent Africa, a lawless and rapacious Mexico—these are all the ways in which the outcome of history is rendered into a simply moral fable. In postapocalyptic cinema the lawless state of nature no longer appears as a geographical zone that retains the violence of primitive origins but takes the form of the future that we will suffer once the social fabric of civility falls away. The heart of darkness from which we must distance ourselves is no longer a past that is somehow retained elsewhere, what Conrad's Marlow refers to as the "dark places of the earth." It is the future that is now imagined as utterly dehumanized; in the end-times, all the world will be McCarthy's Mexico.

Postapocalyptic cinema presents battle after battle to save the world from various evils. It is this very Manichean narration of humanity versus its threatening others that occludes both humanity's production of moral opposites and the destructive force of that oppositional imaginary. Theodor Adorno might at first appear excessively and unfashionably abstract in his claims about art and politics; his conception of a general and existential mimesis that gives order to a reality too traumatic to be confronted authentically comes close to universalizing a modernist and post-Kantian conception of art as pure form.[27] It is as though there is one history—from enlightenment to modernism—and one human condition that begins with managing the world through myth, followed by the negation of mythic mimesis. It is as though there is a single and tragic history of human life that is at once utterly brutal and damaged, while also harboring weakly utopian intimations of a life not subjected to the brutal mechanization of existence that is the history of reason. The advent of the Anthropocene and the violently general conception of who we are yields a new way to think about Adorno (and other theorists of the human condition); there is such a thing as the human, even if it does not coincide with the species and even if it is a geopolitical rather than natural kind. Two concepts from Adorno are worth revisiting in the light of the Anthropocene. Adorno's claims regarding the history of art and the history of enlightenment enable a way to delimit the anthropos of the Anthropocene and understand the trajectory of a specific aesthetic tradition. Like Barthes, who saw myth as the way in which the political and historical forces of the world were rendered into rigid images, Adorno accepted that what is usually depicted as nature is the outcome of figuration. What makes Adorno's work significant is his insistence that what lies outside the figuration of art is not easily graspable, along with his acute sense of damaged life. Art at once covers over this damage and also—in that very production of a harmonious existence—promises what is out of this world. Faced with the moralizing and hypernormative affirmations of the future of humanity, one might ask whether the task of reading should be primarily critical and demystifying or whether there is some way to intuit what lies beyond the mania of saving our world. Might one think of the Anthropocene and postapocalyptic culture through what Adorno refers to as negative dialectics? The shrill insistence on a single humanity with prima facie right to life drowns out any other conception of existence, and yet all that postapocalyptic yelling compels one to think about all that remains unheard (unless one is listening).

What has come to know itself as the human (especially in the Anthropocene) is given form through the management of nature; we are nothing other than the geopolitics that create the world as that which resists falling into a chaos that is always at the edge of existence. Various forms of critical theory in the twentieth century were critical of this moral image of humanity and sought multiple ways to come to terms with the resistant otherness that had always been given in the forms of savagery, destitution, worldlessness, and mere survival. In an age of extinction, the ways in which we think about humanity and life become ever more crucial, especially when life is at once deployed as that which must be saved, even if the human has formed itself by marking off bare or mere life. Life is what must be redeemed, managed, and sustained, even if humanity has been formed as the being whose existence gives sense and value to life. What thinkers like Adorno, Barthes, Jacques Derrida, and Stiegler enabled was a demystifying critique of the *meaning* of life. Narratives, such as the narrative of the Anthropocene, are productive and not innocently descriptive, and that which is not narratable is either figured ideologically as some heart of darkness beyond all sense or imagined as some impossible plenitude that can only be at the limits of desire. There would, on this account, be a difference between frozen myth (Barthes), metaphysics (Derrida), popular culture (Adorno), or stereotypes (Stiegler), which have a lulling and pacifying effect on existence, and forms of art that try to undo the world. For the European critics of the West, it was the West's own tradition of aesthetics that would signal a play or negativity not assimilable to the machine of reason. For the most part, Western critical theory has played this game on its own terms, imagining that the undoing of Anthropos would come from the high art of the West itself. Adorno saw modernism as a way of drawing attention to the forms that gave sense to an otherwise violently damaged life and in so doing resisted the all-too-palatable productions of pop culture. Stiegler articulated a similar opposition between mass-produced industrial culture, which is stereotypical, and the traumatypes that are created by genuine cinematic auteurs.[28] A cursory reading of Stiegler yields the impression that he, like Barthes and Adorno, considers Western conceptions of humanity on their own problematic terms, with little interest in other aesthetic trajectories that might offer different possibilities of rupture. There is, however, within Stiegler's corpus the sense of different and varied economies of the human. If consciousness is the effect of technics and if it is the storage of memory in technical objects that enables the historical retention of habits and desires, then different modalities of the human would be made possible by different technological histories.[29]

The question I want to pose—especially in the twenty-first century, where we seem to be facing a common tragedy of one damaged world—is whether a quite specific concept of the human is unique (or, rather, parochial) and therefore not at all worthy of the absolute right to life that is assumed in postapocalyptic discourse. What if there were other modes of existence that did not regard the world as a domestication of nature that must then somehow be regained in a posthuman future? What if the scene depicted in *The Counselor*—the all-too-human enjoyment of being an elevated spectator in relation to a nature that is red in tooth and claw—were typical of *the* human condition, where the human is a quite delimited "we"? The human condition would be a quite specific historical geopolitical formation bound up with industries that stabilized nature, both literally and figuratively. Slavery, colonization, industrialization, and agribusiness produce a nature that requires a civilized comportment to render it into a world, a horizon of sense and self-becoming. Only by producing a climate, or nature as a stable environ, can there appear to be that *other* nature at the margin—the repressed nature of nightmarish and inhuman chaos. The Anthropocene produces the human, or anthropos, *both* as the being who altered the earth at a geological level and as the being who recognizes this transformation. One political possibility today is to refuse the term "anthropos" and argue that it is a specific fragment of the human species that mastered and reconfigured the earth as nature and then discovered that nature and humanity were intertwined.[30] Another possibility, and one I will argue for here, is that we keep the term "anthropos," because without the conception of the human condition, without the temporal logic of humanity as beings who distance themselves from nature in order to rediscover their own forming power, there would not be the world as we know it and as it is constantly reproduced.

In *The Counselor*, one might think of the scene of animal violence *not* as capturing an opposition between the inauthentic veneer of civilization and a rapacious state of nature but as a critical reflection on this opposition. It is as if America itself were nothing other than this fantasy of a walled-off space of stability that is threatened by the rapacious underbelly of that other humanity that is just across the border. *The Counselor* would be *about* the imaginary Mexico that is fantasmatically and cinematically divided from an ideal of America as a land of free and fully humanist self-formation. Without the mythic alterity of McCarthy's Mexico, there would be no America—no central "we" who can always look with horror at what might happen were our world to fall away. Rather than say that Mexico represents (or suffers from) the unmediated horrors of life and that without the wall between us and Mexico we would fall into the end of the world, one might see *The Counselor* (like *The Road*) as a dystopian depiction of a walled-in humanity. Rather than think of this as an *ideology*, where others are demonized and dehumanized, it is more accurate to think of such structures as the world itself—not simply a mindset or worldview but the very structure that assembles bodies and space. The world that is now being threatened with an end is the world that has divided the globe between stability and fragility, between humanity and its others. Humanity is a visceral, cinematic, and institutional structure that gets composed with every experience of *our* world being saved from *them*.

The human is produced by a series of industries that render life into world (a horizon or sense of possibility) versus worldlessness; such industries also require and produce the end of the world—the assumption and orientation that without mediation, elevation, sensemaking, and self-recognition, we would no longer be human. In *The Counselor* it is the dark world of drug dealing that produces a space of precarity outside the "we" of urban security; but the drug trade is not an exceptional or marginal corruption within capitalism. Global capitalism in general produces and relies on spaces of fragility and volatility. Slave labor, pollution, the export of waste, and resource extraction continue long histories of colonization that enabled spaces of luxury, private consumption, and ease that became constitutive of the human. Anthropos is, as Anthropocene discourse recognizes, the being who transforms the earth into a world and then recognizes that transformation, ultimately imagining any other life as the end of the world. Rather than see texts such as *The Counselor* or *Heart of Darkness* as depoliticizing narratives that depict the outside of the West as the nightmare from which civilized life has distanced itself, it might be better to see McCarthy's Mexico or Conrad's Africa as the quite necessary scene of the end of the world that is intrinsic to the world. *The Counselor*, *Heart of Darkness*, and more explicitly end-of-world fictions like *The Road* are ultimately concerned with a certain type of world: the stabilized and walled-in world of the affluent West. This world is *the world*. It is other than Mexico, walled off from the threat of falling into inhumanity, gazing on its global others as so many hearts of darkness. It is a world that must constantly display its own end as a future possibility of worldlessness and dispersal. This world is formed through a specific history of visual technologies and a series of myths and fantasies attached to images.

To be human is not only to view a world of framed and edited images, not only to manufacture nature, but also to become aware of ourselves as world makers. This definitively human history of image recognition begins at least with Plato, where we must not simply view images but also question their source and then turn the soul around to the origin that enables all images;[31] we must not simply watch the world unfold but become aware of ourselves as auteurs.[32] Kant argues that *practically* we must view nature as if it were created in harmony with our sense of order and virtue and yet recognize that this transcendental order is not nature's own but an effect of our powers of synthesis.[33] Nietzsche defined the fall, and perhaps origin, of humanity by way of its relation to theatrical viewing: the ancient Greeks were once capable of viewing life in its full intensity, enjoying the festive cruelty of existence. With morality, order, and language, the Dionysian force of life was increasingly subjected to systematization, not encountered in its complexity but judged by way of a "higher world" that rendered this world guilty.[34] Nietzsche's ideal viewer is someone like Kurtz in *Heart of Darkness* or Malkina (Cameron Diaz) in *The Counselor*—someone who has not yet fallen into the moralizing framework of demanding that images be parsed into good and evil.

There is a long tradition in feminist and Marxist criticism (and cultural studies more generally) of questioning the ways in which what is presented as natural, universal, or comprising *the* human condition is *really* an outcome of quite specific economic and sexual systems of violence. Fredric Jameson's conception of ideology, which borrows from Lacanian psychoanalysis and Adorno's Marxism, defines ideology as the imaginary form in which individuals live the relation between the symbolic and the real—that is, our imaginary social structures are never reality itself (which resists symbolization absolutely). It is the gap between the symbolization of the world and what is outside symbolization that is lived ideologically.[35] Life is not the beautiful humanist whole that is promised by all the images we consume; ideology is the way in which this gap is lived. Despite the abstraction of this definition, it sharpens the sense in which ideology might be thought of less as a mindset or purely ideal phenomenon and instead as the way in which the actual world of bodies and spaces includes fictions, images, and fantasies as constitutive of its relations. Without end-of-world dramas, there is no world that is held together by institutions that are focused entirely on averting the apparent disaster of *us* becoming *them*. Naomi Klein has referred to "disaster capitalism," which is not only the opportunistic gouging and exploitation that follows from "natural" disasters but also the industries that produce a world where whatever is *not us* is perceived as potentially catastrophic and then ripe for capitalist salvation.[36] Disaster capitalism cannot survive without the production of spaces that must be walled off from spaces of imagined civility and then mined for resources. Conrad's Africa and McCarthy's Mexico would be ways of configuring a relation to otherness in representational form, thereby occluding the more powerful alterity—the raw "not us"—that composes the world. But such places and relations to otherness are not representations; ideology is not merely an idea but the lived relation between the symbolic order and the real, the way in which otherness is experienced and managed. In end-of-world culture, the real conditions of volatility, resource depletion, capitalist barbarism, and racial violence are lived and managed in the heroic narratives of saving the world *from them*.

The Counselor—like so many narratives about the thin veneer of civilization—seems to be rather unfashionably existential, rather than political, suggesting something horrific per se about life. The image of Malkina taking delight in two animals fighting to the death appears as if it were an authentic and uncensored relation to a world that (if we were honest and not coddled by bourgeois timidity) would be able to enjoy the sheer intensity of existence. Like most of McCarthy's fiction, The Counselor depicts what happens when the thin veil of urbanity is lifted. Not only does it suggest an originary and natural violence that is the way of the world; it also frames this violence from the point of view of spectator glee—a motif that is mirrored both at the end of the film when the counselor receives a DVD of what we assume is the dismemberment of his lover and in the middle of the film when Malkina mounts a car windshield, spreads her legs, and displays what we assume (from the expression of the car's two male passengers) to be the utterly horrific presentation of her genitalia. Dismemberment and female genitalia appear to be the base conditions from which man temporarily but vainly seeks to save himself. In McCarthy's most explicit text about the end of the world, *The Road*, father and son wander a depleted landscape, with the father haunted by the memory of the child's mother, who (again authentically) saw bringing a life into the world as an unmitigated harm and who chose to kill herself rather than survive in a world that was pure violence.

The idea of the end of the world as the revelation of the true horror of existence that had been covered over by civility might at first appear to be the counternarrative to postapocalyptic hyperhumanism. Most end-of-world films are oriented toward saving the world, assuming humanity's prima facie right to life. Lars von Trier's *Melancholia* (2011) is a notable exception and is closer to *The Counselor*, *The Road*, and *Heart of Darkness* in its existential affirmation of the authenticity of refusing the bourgeois attachment to life in its modern, privatized, domesticated normalization. Such antihumanist texts can be read as existential and therefore depoliticizing in their positing of a naturally violent life, with a simple opposition between civility and life, precluding the possibility of more complex accounts of what counts as civilization or the human. If one were to accept the verdict of Justine from *Melancholia* that "the earth is evil," there would be little room for thinking about the geopolitics of evil. There is, though, another way in which these texts frame and politicize just this problem: the cinematic mythology of the West is bound up with a long history of institutions and disciplines that create the walled-off space of domestic security, while exporting their volatilities to those zones that would then figure as spaces of worldlessness, violence, and evil. It makes sense within the world of *Melancholia*—the world of advertising, hyperconsumption, and commodification—that the planet itself might seem to be worthy of meeting its end. The nihilism that celebrates the end of this evil earth nevertheless opens a space beyond saving or reforming the world; ending this world, declaring the earth to be evil, and finding no space to escape might open the question of the toxic composition of the present. *Melancholia* is about the end of the world, but it significantly opens with a wedding and stages the end of the world as a familial drama. The father—who cannot face the possibility of the nonbeing of the world—kills himself, leaving his wife, his sister-in-law, and his child to huddle into a makeshift enclosure as the planet meets its death. The end of the world, and the joyous affirmation of the world's end as the end of evil, is intertwined with the enclosure and hyperconsumption of the family. This staging of the end of the world from within the familial scene of late capitalism is a (possibly unwitting) diagnosis of the sexual biopolitics of postapocalyptic culture.

What appears as the world, along with the humanity that deems itself to be the only agent worthy of inheriting that earth, is the outcome of the sex-gender-race system. The domestic sphere is made possible by the sexual contract,[37] but that familial complex that produces the oedipal triangle is in turn made possible by slavery and colonization and the production of state societies that overcode tribal and nomadic forms.[38] Anyone who has read nineteenth-century fiction or the feminist criticism that attaches to the European novel in general knows only too well that the narrative of humanist becoming is inextricably bound up with figurations of gender and race. The novel is in part romance and in part bildungsroman. But becoming who one ought to be requires sexual coupling, and sexual coupling presupposes sexed subjects whose world is their playground. A saintly white femininity holds the world together, always threatened by a femininity that is a dark continent.[39] In *The Counselor* the bloodthirsty, car-humping Malkina is contrasted with the saintly Laura (Penelope Cruz); in *Heart of Darkness* a similar opposition is figured between Kurtz's white European intended, to whom Marlow finds himself compelled to lie, and the African woman whom Marlow describes as "a wild and gorgeous apparition of a woman."[40] Woman is not quite a simple other, but complex figurations of gender are the ways in which fantasies of otherness play out. Bodies are racialized by being oversexed *and* by being nothing more than ungendered flesh.[41] Without the racial and colonial industries of the bourgeois family, there is no heteronormativity in its current form; but without the libidinal investment in bodies and the sexualization of flesh, the world in its current raced and gendered form does not exist. End-of-world films rely heavily on holding the world together by way of holding the family together, but that figure of the family is only possible because of a prior geopolitical history.

Melancholia opens with a wedding that typifies a world at its end: hyperconsumption and excess are figured by a limousine too large to negotiate a turn in the road and a marriage celebration featuring ad executives eager to use the occasion to cut deals. The marriage is a scene of excess and nihilism that gives way to the bride Justine's increased distance from the proceedings and her embrace of the end: "The earth is evil." Her sister, by contrast, seeks to hold on to the world and does so until the end, where they erect a magic cave (a makeshift wooden tepee) that houses them until the planet's end. The sisters repeat the division between the authenticity of facing the truly horrific forces of life and the lie of domesticity. In *Melancholia* there is a geopolitical sense that this world of civility that relies on occluding the intensity of life is bound up with a U.S.-centered form of expropriating capitalism. The world will end with ad executives fighting to make one last deal. The earth's destruction becomes one more cinematic event, with Claire's husband, John, obsessively viewing the approaching planetary collision through a telescope until he kills himself rather than face the end. For all its unremarkable cliché, it is perhaps worth revisiting this sexual opposition between a femininity that (however naively) holds on to social and domestic order in the face of barbarism and a demonic image of a woman who will lure civilized men into the abyss. *Melancholia* seems to embrace Justine's nihilist contempt for the earth, which is set against a world of hyperconsumption, in a house where Brueghel hangs on the wall, reduced to so much interior design. For all its authentic contempt for the world of advertising and spectator capitalism, *Melancholia* gives its authentic point of view to the individual (Justine) whose depressive detachment from the world allows her to embrace the truth of death. There is a strong critique of the framing and management of disaster that runs throughout the film, but the only alternative to the corporate hedonism that cannot face the intensity of suffering is the isolated depression of Justine. She, like Conrad's Kurtz in *Heart of Darkness*, appears to have kicked herself loose of the earth, "kicked the very earth to pieces."[42] The apparent opposition that is heavily racialized in *Heart of Darkness* is, in *Melancholia*, played out within the white bourgeois private sphere. One either lives the lie of white civility or embraces the dark intensity of existence.

What makes *The Counselor*'s heavily clichéd use of the sexualization and racialization of the border between civility and barbarism so interesting is its articulation in the current political climate, where I use the word "climate" in a double sense. Imagine that it once might have been feasible to sustain the existential or metaphysical notion that there is something like humanity that has only survived by not paying too much attention to the utter horrors of *life*; it would follow that a certain inauthentic delusional state would be required simply to live on and that beneath the edifice and facade of civilization is the sheer barbarism of the way we *really* are. That notion is no longer feasible; it is civility as such—industrialization, technology, hyperconsumption—that appears to have led to conditions of impending doom for us all and not only for those whom the West has glibly allowed to be collateral damage for the sake of a higher idea. In a film that depicts the relation between the United States and Mexico as a fragile border between the veneer of civility and the existential brutality of the real, the security and nonviolence of the United States is the inauthentic fabrication that occludes the horror of the real. What makes this aspect of the film so *impolitic* is that this early scene of supposedly natural violence establishes a point of view from which we view the geopolitical opposition between a space of protective legality versus outlying regions of brutal vulnerability as simply the way things are, the way things would be if not for the masking of violence by delusions of civility. Politics is, after all, a sense that our existence is relational, dependent on the networks that bring us into being. To see politics as a privileged delusion that would fall away if one were to look too closely at the world seems to be the passively nihilist assumption of *The Counselor*, a film that is utterly at odds with the hyperpolitics of postapocalyptic cinema, which also has its implicit cinematic mode.

Postapocalyptic cinema's framing moralism depicts humanity as saving itself from an end of the world that looks very much like *The Counselor*'s Mexico. One might, then, contrast *The Counselor*'s fatalism with postapocalyptic political narratives of human triumph. What if the statelessness that we imagine to be beyond the border of our world were somehow something like life *not* in an original state but simply life on utterly different terms? I want to suggest that we rethink the way we think about politics and free it from the polity, and certainly from the state. Politics liberated from the polity would approach the unthinkable—imagining the end of this world as the end of *us* but not the end of all possible value. Rather than think of the U.S./Mexico binary as an opposition between *the* world and its end, one might think of existence beyond the fetishized attachment to *the world* that is set off from worldlessness. More specifically, I want to suggest that we deeply question the commitment to cinematic politics that characterizes postapocalyptic cinema and Anthropocene discourse. Why do we imagine the absence of a form of cinematic technology as the end of the world? Why do we think of humans deprived of the state form as less than human?

What Is Unthinkable?

One might define unthinkability in terms of the habits and expectations that compose our very being. One of the major struggles with comprehending climate change might well be the extent to which all we do relies on planet-destroying technologies, while those same technologies of ease narrow our day-to-day vision and make the global effects of what we do unthinkable. Our smartphones keep us updated on friends' dining and exercise habits, the stock market, election results, our heart rate, our sleep rhythms, the daily forecast, and celebrity gossip, but there's no daily alert of planetary change, even if the melting of ice caps and extreme events make it into news alerts. We are at once aware of the globe through the technologies that damage the planet while also being given a quite specific apprehension of the whole. We might think of this as a political unthinkability, as an inability to have the imaginative reach to accept that something is happening because it lies beyond the day-to-day metrics and desires of the polity that houses our being. What is politically unthinkable has partly to do with our body's politically composed temporality; saving the earth for our children is the major future imperative. Saving the world is saving the world of our own imagining but not other worlds.

There is something classically phenomenological about postapocalyptic cinema. How much can we imagine losing before we have reached the end of the world? *The Day after Tomorrow* saves humanity by securing an exit that enables a final view of Earth from an international space station. *Interstellar* journeys through wormholes to save humanity from its resource-depleted present. The question of who or what is worth saving hums in the background of end-of-world cinema, but the question of how much we save and how much we sacrifice increasingly intrudes on everyday life in a world of climate change. It is always assumed that we save our own; we save who we are. The notion that *other* life might continue is no solace at all. End-of-world epics are about just how much of ourselves we are willing to forgo in order to save who we are.

What is obviously and flagrantly political in postapocalyptic cinema is that the extent to which the world that must be saved is political in the narrowest of senses, bound to the polity that is the extension of the familial form. Postapocalyptic cinema is profoundly majoritarian; beginning with the end form of our existence, we play at thought experiments with what we might be able to change. And it seems—as always—we might lament the loss of worlds, but what we cannot imagine is that there really could be anything other than this world. This majoritarian form, in turn, is cinematic; without the geopolitical and private forms that allow us to view ourselves as fragments of humanity in general, life is not worth living. The "we" of postapocalyptic culture in the twenty-first-century Anthropocene produces anthropos through various technologies of global spectatorship; if we are suddenly deprived of quite specific technological platforms and the global reach they enable, we have reached the end of the world. It is against this unthinking attachment to who we are that we need to confront the unthinkable. Is it possible to consider how much our survival requires that we do not think and that we do not confront the unthinkable?

What Would You Do and Who Would You Kill in Order to Save the World?

We are the effects of a particular industry of cultural production and the technological forms of memory that generate the human. Literature and cinema are not reflections, expressions, or interrogations of who we are; there is no "we" outside the archive. There are, however, different ways in which one composes and imagines what counts as an archive. The archival comportment of Anthropocene humanism is cinematic—a subject is defined as human insofar as their individual point of view encompasses the globe and recognizes every other being as viewing the same totality. We are capable of viewing, recognizing, sympathizing, and managing, as well as saving, the rest of the world. What must be avoided at all costs is not the loss of *life* but the loss of *this* life grounded in a first-person view of the globe.

One of the many ways in which this unthinkable loss of who we are (as beings of spectacle) has been depicted is in the possibility of zombification, which is—of course—the extreme loss of world, relations, and political being. The reduction to mere life is the loss of first-person point of view; zombies are simple response mechanisms, beings who act not according to who they are but without decision or identity. A lot has been written about zombies and the complex racial dynamics of the history and politics of Hollywood's use of zombies. Here, I draw attention to one feature only: the absence of interiority and the utter horror of being nothing more than the immediacy of mere life. Even when films are not explicitly about zombies, the end of the world is always about a situation in which we have lost who we are, either because a pandemic has altered those affective aspects of human existence that led to the violence constitutive of the world, such as in Oliver Hirschbiegel's *The Invasion* (2007), or because resource depletion has reduced us to dependent or nomadic hordes (e.g., *Mad Max: Fury Road*). We may have destroyed the world, but the task ahead is to save the world rather than become other than who we are. I would die rather than see the end of my own kind, my world.

The Allegory of Extinction versus the Irony of Extinction

This brings me to a film that not only repeats the existential trauma of the end of the world but also interrogates the metaphysical parochialism of saving who we are. Jordan Peele's *Us* (2019) at first appears to be a heavy-handed allegory—as does Peele's earlier *Get Out* (2017), in which wealthy white socialites steal the bodies of young talented Black lives in order to live on. The two dimensions of *Us* include an allegory of an uprising of the world's tethered (the world of doppelgangers) and a final irony in which one needs to kill one's own self in order to live in the world. *Get Out* is also allegorical and ironic (where we might think of irony, in Paul de Man's sense, as that point at which there is nothing other than inscription, no ground or foundation that would give sense to the differences that compose the world).[43] The harnessing of Black bodies for the sake of white affluence is in part an allegory, but there is also a stunningly existential moment in *Get Out* where the Black maid Georgina (Betty Gabriel) sheds a tear, as if the body were rebelling against its theft. Who is crying? Georgina's body has been used as the vehicle to keep the grandmother alive, and yet this same flesh resists the white humanization that composes its personhood.

The body has become "sentient flesh."[44] Even though Georgina's body has been stolen to keep an elderly white grandmother alive, there is a resistance of the body *against who it is, against a subjectivity that is not its own*. Flesh itself resists, destroying the very coherence of borders between "us" and "them"—at once suggesting that there is no limit to anti-Blackness while also affirming the persistence and power of flesh against the impoverished forms of personhood that compose the world.

In *Us* an allegorical dimension is also coupled with the metaphysical problem of attachment to who one is. *Us* depicts an America of affluence and middle-class ease that relies on a tethered underworld. Beneath the surface of the earth, each human being has a double who was originally brought into existence for the sake of maintaining the world. That project of an enslaved underclass has failed, and the doubles are now buried and forgotten. The doubles who return to the surface are repressed, voiceless, and—like zombies—oddly generic replicas of who we are. On their annual beach holiday, an upwardly mobile Black family find themselves terrorized by their doppelgangers, who appear at first as a hand-holding family in red jumpsuits on the driveway of the family's holiday home. The red jumpsuits mirror the film's opening, which begins with an advertisement for Hands across America—a charity campaign to end homelessness that featured cutout red human figures. The doubles, it becomes apparent, replicate the entire population of America, all dressed in red jumpsuits. After the family free themselves from their home entrapment, they emerge into a world in which the media is struggling to report the uprising. Later scenes show masses of red-jumpsuit-wearing doubles *holding hands across America*. There is a clearly allegorical sense in which an America that imagined itself as domestically protected—everyone in a home—becomes not only imprisoned in its own image of itself but also reduced to the figures of generic humanity.

There is, in addition to the powerful political allegory, a far more important existential or ironic dimension of *Us*, and it has to do with the constitutive question of what you would do and who you would kill in order to save the world. In order to survive, and in order to save herself and her family, Adelaide (Lupita Nyong'o) has to kill the doubles of her own children. She looks at the faces of children who are identical to those she is striving to save and kills them. Eventually, she kills her own double. This narrative arc of the murder of one's double can still be read allegorically, either as the destruction of one's evil demonic other (a classic doppelganger motif) or, politically, as the Black middle-class woman killing her repressed, outraged, and enslaved tethered self in order to survive in this world. One might think of this as an allegory of social death;[45] in order for Black life to continue in this world, one either goes through a thousand tiny deaths, denying one's existence every minute of the day, or one destroys one's world. This allegorical dimension leads to an existential problem; we have followed the narrative arc and watched the central character finally triumph by killing her double, only to find—in the movie's twist—that the opposite is the case. One of the early scenes shows Adelaide as a young girl getting lost at a beach carnival. At the film's end, it is revealed that her brief disappearance—which also caused her to lose the ability to speak—was actually a moment of substitution. Her double has been assuming the life of the original, succeeding in taking on her voice, with the original Adelaide losing voice. Again, there's an allegorical dimension—what appears as an originally moral and ontological distinction between the good human original and her evil double turns out to be the effect of the lives they had the fortune or misfortune to lead. In short, one might read the entire film as an allegory of the dehumanizing effects of enslavement and slavery's aftermath. Such an explanation is powerful and necessary, but it situates slavery as an event within history that might be depicted allegorically, placing the viewer outside the events that can then be judged morally.

What if slavery and destroying those who are *not us* were constitutive of the hand-holding and home-loving humanity that is at the heart of saving the world? The allegory of the untethered as the unacknowledged underclass and aftermath of slavery that we can view with a sense of liberal guilt is accompanied by an irony that destroys this distance. To become who we are, we destroy what is *not us*. The very condition for viewing this film and enjoying its political allegory is the death and annihilation of a population of tethered others whose existence would destroy the world. We kill what is *not us* in order to save the world. This is true in a barbarically literal sense; the day-to-day lives of the world that is constantly saved in postapocalyptic cinema require the ongoing death of so many others. It is also true at an existential level, where the very sense of *us* requires the ongoing loss of so many worlds.

The cinematic moral aesthetic

The end of the world is at once something we avoid at all costs *and* a spectacle that we repeat with stunning monotony. Despite the manifest appearance of so many world-ending films, and the now commonplace critical truism that it is easier to imagine the end of the world than the end of capitalism, the end of the world is rarely depicted. The supposed and often rehearsed end of the world is not a positive state but an anxious negation of what the hyperaffluent West assumes to be essentially human. How much mass media, hyperconsumption, and dehumanization of others would we have to lose before we become *like them*? In many ways, this humanity that cannot imagine its nonbeing is bound up with a cinematic morality. It is by viewing the rest of the world as not quite like us and yet worthy of being saved that humanity constitutes itself as the agent of history, burdened with holding on to the moral fragments of its past for the sake of a global future. Humanity is not so much a concept or idea as it is a set of viewing and managerial practices. Taking account of the rest of the globe ranges from colonization, slavery, industrial agriculture, and global finance to centuries of realist aesthetics that offer the world as so much near likeness to be viewed from the comfort of one's own private space. The world is made possible by the vision and framing of those who are not us. This explains why postapocalyptic cinema is always a form of premourning, taking objects from our present—from baseball caps and records (in *Oblivion*) to the Statue of Liberty (in *Planet of the Apes*)—and showing them both *within* a panorama of meaning and also *as if* they were cut off, merely existing.

To be human is to be a cinematic animal. Nowhere is this more evident than in *Blade Runner 2049*, where the narrative centers on the existential border between human and nonhuman. K (Ryan Gosling) is led to believe that he is human by way of a relation to a singular object—a small figurine of a horse—and the fragmentary, nonlinear nature of his memory. If the object exists, he speculates, then he is a real human whose sense of self is composed from this world. We learn, however, that this constitutive memory is a digital-media project, designed on-screen by a gifted individual cut off from the world. The narrative trajectory turns on the opposition between a memory that is merely cinematic and digital versus a memory that would be tied to this world and its objects; but that opposition itself is made possible by a cinematic comportment. To be human is to be attached to the things that make us who we are and the flashbacks to key moments that individuate us. The images and things that compose our desire—and therefore who we are—are quite explicitly in *Blade Runner 2049* products of late industrial capitalism. Stiegler has referred to this as the pro-letarianization of sensibility, where our comportment to the world and the desires that constitute who we are, are produced entirely by large corporations, no longer enabling any of the consumers of these images and fantasies to take up a productive relation to a culture's stereotypes.[46] Stiegler ties this historical tendency back to arche-cinema as the very genesis of the human. Once desires are given external material form—whether that be cave painting or cinema—one can experience the desires of others, allowing those desires to be sustained and repeated through time. For Stiegler this exosomatic production of the human transforms the political question at the heart of Western philosophy: What makes life worth living? We cannot refer to some human nature that would provide a foundation for values and worthiness. Not only is the human "we" depen-dent on the norms that give coherence and reason to the lives and decisions we make over time, but the time of our lives is also made possible through what Stiegler refers to as tertiary memory. Without the music, images, stories, and things that mark out the time of our lives, there is no "we."[47] The "us" or "we" that is necessarily constituted through any norma-tive life is formed through desires and relations that are made possible by technologies. The "we" that seeks to save itself in end-of-world culture is a "we" composed from looking, reading, and listening by way of increasingly private technologies that open out to the globe. Those very technologies that compose world-disclosing humanity in long and complex circuits can *also* produce an end. The human is both essentially cinematic *and* prone to destruction by way of cinema. It is only through the relations of technology that we become individuated as the desiring beings we are. Those same technologies can also be short-circuited if the attachment to who we are becomes nothing more than repetition of the same.

Postapocalyptic cinema in its current form tends to reduce narrative arcs to the confirmation of who we already are, allowing disaster to provide a means for heroic triumph over all that is not us. There are hints of a more disruptive or traumatic cinematic pleasure, where all that has called itself human takes up a point of view on itself. I have suggested that *The Counselor* makes evident the ways in which an idea of Mexico stands for a nonworld of inhuman rapacity that, at all costs, must be walled off to save who we are; the "we" that sets itself apart from Mexico is constituted through its enjoyment of viewing and managing violence that is always elsewhere. In an even more profound manner, the cinema of Jordan Peele, especially *Us*, places this constitution of the human within a broader geopolitical milieu of racial capitalism. The United States ("us") survives by way of the circulation of images of domestic enclosure, including *Us*'s early depiction of Hands across America—a "color-blind" campaign that will have us all blessed with a home of our own. The safely walled-in home *and* the image of the generic human community become a nightmare that will destroy *us*. It turns out that the other who seeks to rob us of our domestic enjoyment is also the repressed condition, the underbelly, of who we are.

Survival and Pleasure

In one of philosophy's most famous scenes, bodies are chained in a cave, capable only of viewing shadows cast on the cave's wall; they struggle and resist being turned toward the light and the source of images. Plato's cave allegory in *The Republic* makes a distinction between merely existing and existing rationally, and does so by way of two modes of looking: being entranced by the immediacy of the shadows or turning toward the light that projects images. In this primal scene, a distinction is marked between captivated life—being seduced by what merely appears—and reflective life, a life in which some type of conversion has elevated the soul or turned the soul around.

Picture men dwelling in a sort of subterranean cavern with a long entrance open to the light on its entire width. Conceive them as having their legs and necks fettered from childhood, so that they remain in the same spot, able to look forward only, and prevented by the fetters from turning their heads. Picture further the light from a fire burning higher up and at a distance behind them, and between the fire and the prisoners and above them a road along which a low wall has been built, as the exhibitors of puppet shows have partitions before the men themselves, above which they show the puppets. . . .

See also, then, men carrying past the wall implements of all kinds that rise above the wall, and human images and shapes of animals as well, wrought in stone and wood and every material, some of these bearers presumably speaking and others silent. . . .

Consider, then, what would be the manner of the release and healing from these bonds and this folly if in the course of nature something of this sort should happen to them. When one was freed from his fetters and compelled to stand up suddenly and turn his head around and walk and to lift up his eyes to the light, and in doing all this felt pain and, because of the dazzle and glitter of the light, was unable to discern the objects whose shadows he formerly saw, what do you suppose would be his answer if someone told him that what he had seen before was all a cheat and an illusion, but that now, being nearer to reality and turned toward more real things, he saw more truly? And if also one should point out to him each of the passing objects and constrain him by questions to say what it is, do you not think that he would be at a loss and that he would regard what he formerly saw as more real than the things now pointed out to him?[48]

Not only is captivation by images depicted as prior to enlightenment; there is also a resistance to turning toward the light accompanied by a background sense that there are others who are the authors of the play of shadows. This is not a merely philosophical concern but becomes increasingly urgent in the twenty-first century. Alongside what we might refer to as biopolitics in its strict sense—where governments manage the life of their population—there is also a broad cultural concern regarding a fall back into mere existence. We are, as Sylvia Wynter has argued, continuing a long narrative of human reason and its perils but now operating with the sense of humanity as biocentric:

> The West, over the last five hundred years, has brought the *whole* human species into its *hegemonic*, now purely secular (post-monotheistic, post-civic monohumanist, therefore, itself also transumptively liberal *monohumanist*) model of being *human*. This is the version in whose terms the human has now been redefined, since the nineteenth century, on the *natural scientific model* of a *natural* organism. This is a model that *supposedly* preexists—rather than *coexists* with—all the models of other human societies *and* their religions/cultures. That is, all human societies have their ostensibly natural scientific organic basis, with their religions/cultures being merely superstructural. All the peoples of the world, whatever their religions/cultures, are drawn into the homogenizing global structures that are based on the-model-of-a-natural-organism world-systemic order. This is the enacting of a uniquely secular liberal monohumanist *conception* of the human—Man-as-*homo oeconomicus*—as well as of its rhetorical

overrepresenting of that member-class conception of being human (as if it is the class of classes of being human itself).[49]

It is this problem of life, where one marks a difference between a merely captivated life enslaved to shadows versus a reflective and complex life, that opens up the question of cinema, pleasure, and the end of the world. In Plato the proper soul does not merely view the world's images but takes up a relation to the source of imaging. Although the border between mere life and reflective life is obviously a philosophical distinction, it has just as much force—and increasingly so—in popular culture. Postapocalyptic cinema frequently views the end of the world as a global catastrophe where so many passive others are lost in a war that allows the West to view, manage, and mourn the disaster and then save itself. It is as though every postapocalyptic narrative is ultimately a tale of zombification, in which the worldless fall away in order to allow those blessed with reason and global consciousness to inherit the future. Beyond zombie cinema, and beyond explicit end-of-world disaster epics, distinctions between life and mere life have a far more general purchase in postapocalyptic culture. We appear to be one virus or one tornado away from falling back into merely existing; as soon as what we think of as the social fabric of civilization falls away, we become hordes and masses, scrambling and panicking to exist. These distinctions are increasingly racialized. From the colonizer's gaze on the "new world" as a world of savage immanence to the Anthropocene discourse of global stewardship,[50] there is only one "we," and it is a "we" that defines itself against the horrors of passivity, statelessness, and mere subsistence.

Here is where one might think of the intimate relations among cinema, pleasure, and life. Plato depicts a condition of almost natural slavery in the tendency to be captivated by images; the life worth living is not one in which we are passive recipients.

By the time we get to cinema in the explicit sense, and especially to postapocalyptic cinema, the border between a life bound to immediacy and a life of elevation becomes cinema's very content. Between Plato's depiction of being captivated by shadows projected on a cave wall and twenty-first-century dystopias and anxieties about us all being seduced by images not of our own making (what Stiegler refers to as "proletarianization of sensibility"), there are countless meditations on what makes life worth living that are tied directly to cinematic pleasure and that use metaphors and images of slavery to describe a life that is not actively cinematic.

Plato imagines the enslaved spectators turning around to see the source of images, allowing them then to view the world as having its source of truth elsewhere—not the world itself but the light that illumines the world. After Plato, the elevated human eye does not simply view the source of light for the world but takes up a role in composing the world into a meaningful sequence. The clearest example of such a claim for the cinematic eye is Kant, who not only argues that our everyday experience of the world retains the past, anticipates the future, and marks out a space and time in which events are located; he also ties this process of synthesis to our scientific and aesthetic experience of the world. In terms of scientific experience, Kant argues that we can never experience a law of nature or the order of the cosmos. We nevertheless view the world *as if* it operated according to some intentional order and assume that other individuals similarly presuppose this order.[51] We view history, despite looking back on a trail of wreckage, violence, injustice, and barbarism, *as if* it were progressing toward a final and legitimate peace. We view the beauty of nature *as if* everything were arranged to harmonize with our own sense of proportion. The "I" who perceives the world is, for Kant, not merely a spectator but a spectator who recognizes that the world has been composed. The Kantian subject also realizes that this art of composition only appears to be objective, with the appearance of harmonious objectivity being the same for any possible subject. The world is experienced as real (empirically real) and, upon reflection, transcendentally ideal—harmonious because each subject's synthesizing powers are what enable and yield individuality and are certainly not reducible to individuals. To put this in cinematic terms, although the idea is already highly cinematic, it is as though the world were the outcome of a gifted film producer, who has edited and spliced images for maximal effect; it turns out that the gifted editor is us. It is as though we are viewing a film that we ourselves *would* have made, with the recognition of this making leading to a rational cosmopolitanism. Every rational being would compose a similarly coherent world, but from their own point of view; the same logic would be expressed by each viewer. Even though Kant is making a claim about what it is to view the world as such, for any subject whatever, it is implicit that it is this mode of reason that makes us worthy and moral animals. A certain comportment to the world—one in which I recognize all others as world forming—will lead to what Kant refers to as rational cosmopolitanism.

In the beginning, the world will have been cinematic, unfolding from the common horizon of sense. The philosophical argument for transcendental subjectivity is a formal claim, but it is also a moral imperative. For Kant, to act as if one's world were the outcome of one's decisions would be to act as a member of the kingdom of ends. If we think of ourselves as merely mechanical beings, we would have no sense of what we *might do were the world to follow our own lawful decision-making*. To think of oneself as capable of composing a world of one's own has practical force, generating a sense of awe and respect *not* for who we are but for who we might become. It is our virtual rather than actual existence that constitutes humanity's worth.

While this may be a highly philosophical conception when phrased in Kantian terms, it is an easily discernible feature of postapocalyptic morality. How else could one live in and justify this world if its apparent brutality were not somehow offset by the assumption of a future of felicity? There is already, within Kantian thought and its aftermath, a curious bifurcation of the human; without some sense of what is *not yet*, without some sense of becoming, humanity would be yet one more being within the world. The *idea* of humanity breaks with actuality and yet also gives all those who happen to be human a virtual and absolute right to life. If there is something futural about desire, as such, it is because desire negates a present state for a fulfilment to come. Life in general is only worth living with an orientation to a world that is not yet or not present. But what is the idea or orientation that opens the present? Must it always be tethered to humanity, to us, to who we are or should be?

In his early work, Jacques Derrida referred to the "opening to infinity,"[52] noting the ways in which a presupposed transcendental subject was posited by writers like Husserl and Kant as a fragment in the world that ruptures the world: "Consciousness of confronting the same thing, an object perceived as such, is consciousness of a pure and precultural *we*."[53] Derrida took the terms within the discourse of humanism—ideas such as democracy, justice, and futurity—and intensified their virtual dimension, creating a democracy to come, justice to come, or future to come. No actual democracy can fulfil the promise of the concept of democracy, which always bears a force to be reiterated beyond any current context; the same can be said for all of political philosophy's concepts. Derrida's disruption of the commonsense grasp of who we are is at the end point of a long history of Western metaphysical counterhumanism, in which humans turn away from their natural selves and discover their capacities to transcend any determined or merely natural existence. In so doing, the human maintains itself but only by surpassing and suspending itself.[54] This structure of holding on to who we are while also negating who we are is not simply philosophical but has something generally cinematic and postapocalyptic in its configuration. It is attachment to who *we* are and what *we* might become that gives life meaning—a possible ongoing narrative of fulfilment, especially when we imagine ourselves as capable of sacrificing our life for the sake of who we are. It is the *idea* of humanity, not the world's grubby past, that makes the world worth saving.

Postapocalyptic cinema produces scenes of destruction that allow for the spectacle of planetary catastrophe, while creating a point of view that oversees and saves the fragment of the world tasked with survival. Such narratives intensify what Sylvia Wynter has referred to as monohumanism, a historical and political trajectory that is bound up with narrative as a species-forming event. The "human" of monohumanism has been forged through a narrative tradition that, despite its dynamism and complexity, occludes other possibilities of human existence. This limiting of existence to the narrow range of humanity becomes even more apparent and destructive in an age of planetary catastrophe. Wynter, writing on Derrida's "Ends of Man" and its relation to current diagnoses of climate change, criticizes Derrida for maintaining the assumed "we" of humanism:

Yet, he says, French philosophers have assumed that, as middle-class philosophers, their referent-we (that of Man2) is isomorphic with the *referent-we* in the *horizon of humanity*. I am saying here that the above is the single issue with which global warming and climate instability now confronts us and that we have to replace the ends of the *referent-we* of liberal monohumanist Man2 with the ecumenically human ends of the *referent-we in the horizon of humanity*. We have no choice.

If we take the report put forth by the climate panel in *Time* seriously, what we find is this: the authors of the report, as natural scientists, and also bourgeois subjects, logically assume that the *referent-we*—whose normal behaviors are destroying the habitability of our planet—*is that of the human population as a whole.* The "we" who are destroying the planet in these findings are not understood as *the referent-we of homo oeconomicus* (a "we" that includes themselves/ourselves as bourgeois academics). *Therefore, the proposals that they're going to give for change are going to be devastating!* And most devastating of all for the global poor, who have already begun to pay the greatest price. Devastating, because the proposals made, if nonconsciously so, are made from the perspective of *homo oeconomicus* and its attendant master discipline of economics, whose behavior-regulatory metaphysical telos of mastering Malthusian natural scarcity is precisely the *cause* of the problem itself.[55]

The notion of a single life that can be redeemed through the management of a global human totality, with the reasoning human at its center, is—now more than ever—bound up with the scenes of destruction that supposedly only humanity can redeem.

The human (in Wynter's sense of monohumanism) is at once a transgression and suspension of who we are, justifying at the same time who we happen to have been. Because there is one life that precedes us all, there is (it is assumed) a single humanity that will secure *our* future. Postapocalyptic redemption narratives embrace forms of disaster or disruption as the occasion for humanity to find its better and triumphant future self. Meanwhile, modes of orientation that are inhuman and out of this world are rarely considered. When such modes of existence are occasionally considered, they are invariably deemed to be

unworthy. Those who are assumed to be *not us*, those whose existence seems to mirror the conditions that we imagine as the end
of the world, seem to be poor in world in the Heideggerian sense.
Occasionally, such an existence is somewhat alluring, as with
Avatar's imagined world of neural interconnectedness, but the
valorized other ultimately secures the future *for us* (we humans).
As Hee-Jung S. Joo argues, racialized others are either vehicles for
the redemption of whiteness or those whose world stands for the
end of the world.[56] Within the racialized tradition of viewing the
world as human for us all while nevertheless assuming the worldlessness of others, there is a division between the global look
of encompassing recognition and a fantasy of childlike, savage,
or animal immediacy. In *Avatar* the rapacious and plundering
Americans are contrasted unfavorably with the nature-attuned
Na'vi, but it is an American who takes on the mission of admir-
ing and saving the Na'vi. There is something alluring about the
mythic worldlessness of others, and yet that lure, more often
than not, intensifies the value of being worldly enough to admire
the simplicity and innocence of others while recognizing humanity proper as blessed with a higher sense of the order of things.

Kant briefly imagines what it might be like simply to see
the world—not as if it were composed *for us* but simply as it
is. This would be a form of wild or savage vision. In his essay
on materiality in Kant, Paul de Man notes that the form of
poetic seeing that was akin to savage vision for Kant provided
a more radical sublime, one that would not see the world as if it
were built for us but would be a form of mere seeing. De Man
quotes Kant's *Lectures on Logic*: "If a savage sees a house from a
distance, for example, with whose use he is not acquainted, he
admittedly has before him in his representation the very same
object as someone else who is acquainted with it determinately
as a dwelling established for men. But as to form, this cogni-
tion of one and the same object is different in the two. With

the one it is mere intuition, with the other it is intuition and concept at the same time." De Man then notes that "the poet who sees the heavens as a vault is clearly like the savage, and unlike Wordsworth. He does not see prior to dwelling, but merely sees."[57] Such conceptions of a pure seeing that is not yet burdened with meaning, purpose, and ownness have a curious place in Western aesthetics, occasionally valorized as sublime and often romanticized as being childlike, primitive, or essentially transgressive. At its most extreme, Sartrean existentialism will affirm consciousness as pure freedom, nothing other than the negation of the fixity of mere being.[58] To look is to be a subject. (To be looked at is to be an object, a thing within the world without sense of world.) While Sartre aligned the pure transcendence of the subject with humanism and elevated the pure gaze over the object, thinkers from Franz Fanon onward recognized the ways in which the overseeing gaze of mastery was bound up with race, colonization, and reification.[59] Even when notions of unmediated intuition are regarded as redemptive rather than merely savage—even when it is childlike anti-self-consciousness rather than zombification that is used to depict mere seeing—it is nevertheless the consciousness that takes up a relation to immediacy that is deemed to be properly human.[60]

To recognize the world, and to be rich in world, is to be *other than* any given or determined nature. It is, to follow Stiegler, a recognition of the fault of Epimetheus. All other beings were given a quality, but because Epimetheus forgot to give humans a nature (the fault of Epimetheus), it became technics (the Promethean gift of fire) that enabled human becoming.[61] Or as Wynter argues, it is to accept that humans are a "hybrid-auto-instituting-languaging-storytelling species: *bios/mythoi*."[62] There is no such thing as the human in any simple or purely natural sense; the constitutive supplement of myth and technics begins—as so many have argued—with the very first inscriptions.

The more significant problem is the axiology of the relation between natural being and becoming.

One might, following Wynter, think of multiplying the narratives that mark the difference between life and the human modes in which it is lived. Or in a similar manner, think of Stiegler's project of confronting humanity's curious pharmakon, where the means of becoming human are also threats to a life worth living. What postapocalyptic culture makes clear is that humanism lives on by distancing itself from the human. Being *other than* simply human takes various forms: affirmations of one vibrant life without species exceptionalism,[63] valorizations of what was once reduced to rational animality as irreducible to any form of worldly being (Heidegger), a radically historical sense of all the contingent ways in which humanity is produced by forms of knowledge (Foucault), or a refusal of the entire humanist project and its negation.[64] It matters how one thinks about suspending or overcoming the human. Posthumanism can amount to repeating the long-standing moralism in which it is the white man of reason who saves the world from himself by enhancing himself and becoming other than himself.[65] It can take the form of celebrating all those recent upheavals in thought and life that seem to threaten the human and argue that they offer an opportunity for transformation.[66] Or one might be less optimistic regarding posthuman self-overcoming and insist that the human in all its sentience and self-transcendence has been made possible through anti-Blackness, colonization, and other forms of geo-bio-politics.[67] Human self-exits have been made possible through a long history of self-transcendence defined *against* flesh, savagery, Blackness, and other inhuman inflections. The world that must be saved is never the world of humanity's past but always its redeemed potentiality that it frequently finds through its becoming other for the sake of humanity regained.

4

Bifurcation

Postapocalyptic humanism takes the form of a felix culpa; it is not immediacy itself that is valorized so much as an immediacy that allows humanism to regain its innocence. The fantasy of the new world, whereby we might once again experience the world with childlike wonder, maintains itself in the postapocalyptic imaginary. Rather than affirm the possibility of a world (or nonworld) beyond the human, various forms of worldlessness—the mythic child, animal, or "primitive" who views the world without the weight of the past—become means for the human to find itself again. It is better to have fallen into being human and then regain one's posthuman or cosmic self than to be other than human from the beginning. In *Avatar*, *Mad Max: Fury Road*, and *Black Panther*, the world of acquisitive human tyranny is saved by the embrace of a new world, a world that is new for the white humanism that can restore itself through its beautiful others. Even when there is a fetishization of pure intuition, immediacy, childlike wonder, and the nonhuman innocence of others, postapocalyptic culture's valorization of the unexamined life requires the point of view of an elevated being who can look on innocence with a gaze of wonder and self-worth. What Freud referred to as the "oceanic feeling"[1]—where there is no sense of self separate from the world—becomes an increasingly seductive state of existence as the mechanization and atomization of late capitalism intensifies. But such states of immediacy are, in postapocalyptic culture, invariably situated as precursors or conduits for the redemption of who *we* ultimately are. Jordan Peele's great achievement is to give critical cinematic form to this constitutive cannibalism of the other at the heart of who we are. *Us* depicts a world of tethered others whose existence *and* annihilation make who we are possible. *Get Out* depicts the allegory of decaying white bodies taking over the vibrancy of young, gifted, and Black persons and (like *Us*) adds to the allegory of cannibalization the metaphysical dimension of the irrational and world-destroying attachment to who we are. We are those beings who become aware of our loss of innocence, gaze longingly on the vibrancy of others, and then save their world in order to maintain who we are—not beings of innocence and immediacy but those who can look on mere life as a new world and horizon of opportunity.

Bifurcation and World

Much has been written about Kant's distinction between European freedom, which is oriented to a concept, and a merely savage freedom oriented to the immediacy of this world.[2] Even when not explicitly racialized, the bifurcation between reflective consciousness and mere existence ties rational cosmopolitanism to racial capitalism. The distinction between mere existence and a properly human capacity for transcendence structured the gaze of settlers and enslavers, who consigned the bodies of non-Europeans to a level of being not quite human and stateless subsistence.[3] One must not simply live and enjoy the world but do so with a sense of who one is among others *of one's own kind*. The range of what counts as kin contracts as it expands. The liberal recognition of all others as (ideally) rational "just like me" is a manifest expansion, but such inclusion is also a reduction and an assimilation. The true challenge would be to grant respect, life, and worth to those who may not be of my kind at all. Donna Haraway has frequently argued for a future where we "make kin, not babies," suggesting that rather than reproducing ourselves, we form new alliances.[4] McKenzie Wark has taken this refusal of one's own kind in a more adventurous dimension, suggesting that we make "kith, not kin." Referring to Haraway's companion species, Wark argues, "They are also kith, with its nebulous senses of the friend, neighbor, local, and the customary. Companion species eat together, parasite off each other, eat each other, but also collude and collaborate with each other."[5]

When postapocalyptic culture imagines the end of the world, its visions of stateless, nomadic, media-deprived peoples who are reduced to the mere ground they stand on fail to consider or imagine what inhuman and cosmic forms of relationality might be possible. It is assumed, both in liberal political theory and the broader policies and panic regarding the end of the world, that the end of rational humanist relationality is the end of humanity. The anthropos may have found itself guilty of having rendered the earth less habitable for most current species, but that very admission intensifies the presupposed "we" of recognition. Because there are now "no lifeboats for the rich," a new unity of common peril comes to the fore.[6] Just how recognition, relationality, and commonality are composed is not a merely figural question; if humanity is defined by way of technological maturity, rational cosmopolitanism, and the complexity of social networks, then most of the non-West *may* appear as being "poor in world." It all depends on what one recognizes as technics, as relationality, as cosmopolitanism. If one thinks of technics in the broadest sense, as an archive of stored memories, and if one thinks of cosmopolitanism as the capacity for a body to see its own life as a fragment of a far more complex and transindividual whole, then there are forms of cosmotechnics well beyond the range of the West. If one defines technics in the manner of some forms of posthumanism—such as Bostrom's "technological maturity" or Kurzweil's "singularity"[7]—then only those forms of cosmopolitanism that tie humans to each other through the archive of human rationalism would count as being rich in world, and only those forms of intelligence that have been formalized through computation would count as the fulfilment of potentiality. There are other forms of relationality beyond the conception of the state as the rich social fabric that renders us fully human. Not all possible modes of existence need to fetishize and valorize human relationality to the point that societies without the grand social fabric of the state appear to be inhuman. One can either imagine other ways of being rich in world or think of what it might be to be "poor in world."

It is possible to imagine highly localized, stateless, and nomadic modes of existence that open to the community through cosmic, mythical, and nonhuman relations. Such forms of world are hinted at in *Avatar* and *Mad Max: Fury Road*, but these pseudo-Indigenous worlds that rely on connections of the earth rather than relations among humans become modes of redemption *for us*. There are counterexamples; perhaps the most provocative is N. K. Jemisin's Broken Earth trilogy, where the central character—far from saving the world—works toward ending the world, precisely because her own kind (who live by experiencing the vibrations of the planet's mineral strata) are enslaved.[8] The question of kindred, and saving one's kindred, is also at the heart of Octavia Butler's writing, not only in *Kindred*, but also in her Xenogenesis trilogy. In *Kindred* Butler poses the question of the limits of one's kind; from twentieth-century Los Angeles, Dana travels back in time to encounter her ancestors, one of whom is a white enslaver and rapist. Kindred, it turns out, are both those whom one would fight to save *and* those who have done all they can to render one worldless. In the Xenogenesis trilogy, Butler broadens the question of kindred and saving one's kind to humanity in general (exposing the ways in which exploring what counts as the human is entwined with parochial racialism). The central character, Lilith, is open to the forms of gene mixing that would save her kind (even if her kind would also be transformed in the process). If Lilith is capable of questioning the integrity and purity of the human, those around her are not. Onkali space travelers save the human world after a global war; they travel space to mine genes of various life-forms, effectively breeding humans into their own future. Rather than simply assume that the worlds of others should seek to save *us*, Butler's central characters—Lilith and Akin—are at once attached to humanity yet struggle with their attachment. They recognize the violence and insensitivity of humankind and yet hold on to the flawed species that is their own. Heightened intelligence and technological maturity might be better served were humanity to concede its territory to invading others, and yet species attachment, or the anxiety about no longer *being us*, haunts Butler's worlds. Butler poses the existential question of attachment to who one is and the ways in which history and violence might render that attachment painful. How might you live if your ongoing existence required the end of the world? In *Kindred* Dana's existence bears within it the aftermath of slavery. In Butler's *Dawn*, being human is world destructive, and saving the world would require abandoning the human. How might the world *look*? Butler's trilogy describes the capture, study, manipulation, and breeding of humans, as if their flesh were unworthy of the right to life, while also being a vehicle for the Onkali's survival. The Onkali save the world and save humanity, but they do so by desiring humans as vehicles for their own future. Humans become objects, not subjects, of enjoyment, raising the question of how one holds on to a world in which one becomes little more than a means to survival and pleasure for others. One of the narrative threads of the trilogy describes coupling between humans and Onkali, in which humans experience affect *without* volition, becoming passive vehicles for nonhuman enjoyment. How might sensus communis be rethought without the pleasures and sensibilities of the subject for whom the world (and many others) is nothing more than the vehicle for one's own elevation?[9]

Butler's description of a spaceship that is also a living being—a living alien ship that consumes humans—also forms the central motif in Jordan Peele's *Nope*. *Nope* ties the existential confrontation with what is *not us* with the cinematic problem of what it is to be a viewed object for a consuming subject. What Butler has explored through a series of novels—the problem of how much we need to abandon of ourselves if there is to be a future—is tied to an even more intensely racialized politics of viewing and consuming in Peele's *Nope*. For Butler, being attached to the human is intertwined with a complex history of violence that is both bifurcated (in *Kindred* between white enslavers and the enslaved) and constitutive; what distinguishes the human in *Dawn* is the tendency toward hierarchy and violence. In *Nope* both of these qualities are tied to vision and the cinematic—the capacity to view is a capacity for objectification and for captivation. The forms of looking that allow humans to render others into animals for consumption and enjoyment have a history. Peele's *Nope* draws attention to one strand of that history, with Hollywood's erasure of its dependence on Black art and labor. This helps to qualify the sense in which the human is cinematic and the sense in which this cinematic nature precedes cinema in its narrow sense. A certain historical and political formation defines humanity through a certain sensibility, as a capacity to look and master a scene that is there *for* human enjoyment. When cinema arrives as an art form, it can both intensify and render explicit the ways in which certain visual comportments are entwined with a geopolitical history of the modern subject and a sense of world mastery. *Nope* draws attention to capitalism's history of industrialized looking; from surveillance cameras to theme parks, the world becomes nothing more than an object to be enjoyed by a subject who is produced as a right to enjoyment. The racial politics of this looking is made even more explicit in *Get Out*, where the ultimate commodity for white enjoyment is the gifted eye of a young Black photographer, Chris Washington (Daniel Kaluuya). His body is photographed and displayed for auction, with the value of his flesh being amplified by his gift for capturing images. Both *Get Out* and *Nope* place the acts of capturing images alongside the problem of being captured. Both tie the power to frame and look to the consumption of bodies that appear to be there only for the white subject's enjoyment. Cinema in the literal sense intersects with a broader cinematic history that is tied to a conception of the human as a subject for whom the world exists as an object of moral enjoyment. Hollywood's repeated depiction of us saving the world has a literary and philosophical prehistory. Without the production of a "we" that is generated from narratives and theories of the sense of the world, there cannot be a postapocalyptic and Anthroposcenic pleasure in saving the world.

Visual Pleasure

There is a link, in Kantian aesthetics, between aesthetic judgment and intersubjectivity; one does not simply take pleasure in the harmony of the world but feels one's own enjoyment as if it would apply to humanity in general. This link has been sustained well beyond Kant in the sensus communis, or ideal of imagined—but not actualized—consensus. We may have given up on arriving at consensus and legitimation, but we converse *as if* we were all moving toward an ideal of agreement.[10] Crucial to this sense of a rational cosmopolitan humanity is not only an open horizon of recognition but also a specific temporality of visual pleasure. For Kant, there is a distinction between the pleasure of reflective judgment and the enjoyment of one's senses. If one simply enjoys something for the bodily sensation it produces, then its value is related only to the specificity of one's body. But if one enjoys something in nature or the art world because of its *form* or the way in which each of its components appears to be arranged in accord with our powers of perception, then one is no longer simply bound to this world but *feels* one's relation to the world in general:

> Thus an aesthetic judgment is that whose determining ground lies in a sensation that is immediately connected with the feeling of pleasure and displeasure. In the aesthetic judgment of sense it is that sensation which is immediately produced by the empirical intuition of the object, in the aesthetic judgment of reflection, however, it is that sensation which the harmonious play of the two faculties of cognition in the power of judgment, imagination and understanding, produces in the subject insofar as in the given representation the faulty of the apprehension of the one and the faculty of presentation of the other are reciprocally expeditious, which relation in such a case produces through this mere form a sensation that is the determining ground of a judgment which for that reason is called aesthetic and as subjective purposiveness (without a concept) is combined with the feeling of pleasure.
>
> The aesthetic judgment of sense contains material purposiveness, the aesthetic judgment of reflection formal purposiveness.[11]

One feels oneself to be more than a simple being within the world; one becomes aware of oneself as one whose very perception composes the world.

As I have already suggested, this conception of the self who has a *world*—a composed, harmonious, and purposive sense of one's space and time—is not at all confined to philosophy. Kant's brief reference to savagery and the conception of one who simply sees the world without a sense of the world's complex time and space is neither confined to philosophy nor to an age when reason and human exceptionalism were unquestioned values. If zombies are those beings who look without really see-ing and exist without really living, then their place in cinema merely brings to the fore what has long been recognized, and problematized, in critical theory: to look is to objectify, and to be the object of a gaze is to be reified. A great deal has been said to complicate this binary, but a kernel of truth remains in the simple version of the politics of the gaze. Even if being the object of another's regard is a pleasure of its own, even if the conception of the pure subject as reifying gaze is a myth, it is a myth that is played out over and over in an actual world that privileges cinematic modes of global cosmopolitanism. The imagined end of the world, or those places imagined as poor in world, are depicted as media bereft, with bodies wandering or staying in place, only negotiating their immediate surrounds, deprived of any grasp of the globe. Just as colonizing visions of the "new world" looked on the "blank spaces" of the globe as historically frozen spots of time awaiting genuinely historical progress toward civilization, so postapocalyptic cinema's dramas of saving the world allow the rest of the globe to be either a resource or collateral damage in a scene of humanist triumph.

Overcoming human actuality—our mere species being—for the sake of becoming who one might be has always been crucial to aesthetic education and elevation.[12] It is also struc-tural to postapocalyptic cinema, where the world that is saved is always *ours*, even if the threat to this world came from the lesser tendencies of our being. Even the piously left-leaning

Kim Stanley Robinson structures his magisterial *Ministry for the Future* by beginning with a devastating heat wave in India, followed by a series of explanations of how various forces—finance capital, ideology, cognitive bias, actor-network theory, the Gini coefficient—conspire to allow 1 percent of the world's population to own, control, and destroy life and the globe. The book's explanatory drive is faithful to Fredric Jameson's imperative to "always historicize."[13] *Ministry for the Future* is an exercise in ideology critique, providing a sweeping judgment of what humanity has been in its capitalist mode, along with a utopian drive to render the future more just and inclusive. Robinson's novel gives form to Jameson's idea that ideology always bears a utopian drive; the capitalist myth of a world that is oriented to justice for all could be a reality.

Ministry for the Future is a compendium of theory, data, and a peculiar form of *speculation*. Where writers like N. K. Jemisin imagine what it might be like to exist in a world that annihilates one's being and where novels like Octavia Butler's *Kindred* or films like *Us* pose questions regarding who the "we" of survival and right to life might be, Robinson uses the voices of Marxism, economics, and other disciplines to save humanity from itself. The central character, Frank, kidnaps a minister from the UN's Ministry for the Future and demands that she do more to save the future, including assassinations and kidnappings of those who are doing all they can to maintain the status quo. Frank, traumatized by the Indian heat wave that opens the novel, has been undertaking assassinations of the world's climate criminals. If Jemisin's form of speculation is to question why one would want to save a world of structural enslavement, thereby speculating about the very composition and worthiness of the world, Robinson uses the master's voice—economics, Marxism, global history—to argue that this world can be saved. Where Jemisin, like Jordan Peele, will confront the existential violence of those who are *not us*, Robinson will forge a narrative and point of view that can distance humanity from itself. Crucial to this bifurcation is a cinematic comportment. One can look at history and the globe with a sense of myriad differences, yet all variations are comprehensible by a roving point of view that synthesizes fragments into a relatively coherent whole. Robinson has sidestepped the problem of the cinematic; the novel assumes and masters its various points of view, never questioning the technologies (of Marxism, economics, climate science, the novel) that make any point of view possible.

There are, then, two broadly different modes of speculation. The first might be thought of as cinematic and humanist, where humanity as it is can be redeemed by a grand vision of history that will see the meek inherit the earth. Who or what humanity is, and the contested nature of its coming into being, is not questioned. The second mode might be thought of as cosmopessimist, where this world that makes one's voice possible is also doing all it can to annihilate and preclude any other world or mode of existence that is *not ours*. If the world that makes living both possible and impossible is not quite ours, this is because the technologies that enable existence always have a history that is irreducible to *us*. Postapocalyptic cinema generally assumes, rather than interrogates, the presupposed "we" of a monotechnological humanity. Most forms of saving the world adopt a normatively cinematic comportment. Unless one is a being who has a technologically mature grasp of the whole, one's life has lesser value. Once one starts to make distinctions among modes of existence, *which is what one must do when one decides to save the world*, and the forms of pleasure and judgment that attach to those modes, it becomes possible to adjudicate forms of life according to the extent to which they meet the standard for elevated perception. To say that Western thought has always found a way to justify enslavement, colonization, and species exceptionalism is unremarkable. What I want to add to that observation is the way in which a cinematic aesthetic has enabled an ongoing and implicit morality and right to life for certain humans. The managerial and biopolitical comportment that produced the enslaved and colonized as so much manipulable flesh was inextricably intertwined with an aesthetics of being other than the mere life that occupied one's gaze.

The Subject Is Cinematic, and Cinema Is Subjective

The valorization of the subject as a synthetic and world-forming power is not a solely philosophical motif. The heroic subject presupposed by contemporary cinema is this subject of expansive vision, aware that to be human is to understand oneself as a fragment of a globe, while also recognizing one's role in composing that global synthesis.

We are all, to some extent, occupying this cinematic comportment today; in fact, the "we" of the Anthropocene is produced through a point of view that looks with alarm at the destructive past and threatened future and yet continues to negotiate how to save and justify this world. Postapocalyptic fictions artfully enable a validation of the long history of species bifurcation by focusing on saving the worthy against the self-interests of the destructive, even if the worthy to be saved are a modified repetition of the same humanity that has colonized and enslaved those portions of the globe who are then viewed as being poor in world. The "we" of the future will be other than those who have destroyed the earth, even if this same "we" once again allows most of the globe to be lost as so much collateral damage in order to save humanity proper. The use of space travel, space colonization, and the colonization of Earth by extraterrestrials in postapocalyptic fiction enables a point of view that can look at the earth (and unified humanity) as that which we ought to save. This seeming unification—a species bound to the earth—is ultimately a bifurcation. This planet-bound humanity turns out to be us, the "we" of global and cinematic humanism, bound to the family and hyperconsumption.

To what extent does my life warrant the sacrifice of other lives? Of course, no one tends to pose the question this way, but I would argue that it is *this* question that is played out over and over again in postapocalyptic cinema. Steven Spielberg's *Saving Private Ryan* (1998)—like Kim Stanley Robinson's *Ministry for the Future*—opens with a scene of such utter devastation that it is hard to imagine any form of moral resolution. The question of what would make a life worth living and how much sacrifice might be justified is posed and answered within the normative frame of the family. Private Ryan needs to be saved because his three brothers have been killed in combat; military administration decides that losing four sons to war would be too much for any mother. After being saved and after watching the death of the captain who led the mission to rescue him, Ryan returns to the graveyard of the war dead decades later. Accompanied by his family, the question of whether his life was worth all that sacrifice is answered in the affirmative. The many wars, conquests, enslavements, and thefts that composed the possibility of the happy nuclear family that closes the film are left out of frame. We—meaning "we humans"—can look at the world and life from on high, with a grand sense of the whole *and* with a sense of what makes life worth living; we have, like those chained in Plato's cave, turned away from simply living and being captivated by what appears and instead have oriented ourselves to what is true in general, for any subject whatever. By locating the truth and universal *within* some conception of humanity, it becomes possible to argue that some forms of life are not worth living, or not as worthy as others. While this distinction appears somewhat abstractly in Plato, given for the most part within the unfolding of a dialogue that will only occasionally tie the life worth living to proper forms of perception, the border between a properly human life and mere life becomes increasingly tied to cinematic time. Western modernity is constituted through a comportment to the *world*—not simply the planet on which we live but a shared horizon of sense. Saving the world is not about saving the planet but saving this relationality—such that when we imagine the end of the world, it is predominantly a scene of fragmentation that marks the end, whether that be the loss of social fabric, the destruction of the shared archive, zombification, or nomadism.

Kant insisted that one looks at the world not only by retaining the past and anticipating the future but also with the sense that the seeming chaos and barbarism of the past is heading to a virtuous future, all the while assuming that others will similarly arrive at this rational cosmopolitanism. That conception of looking back to the past with a sense of a rational and redemptive future to come, with humanity gradually coming together to release itself from petty differences, provides the default narrative structure of postapocalyptic disaster culture. If Kant would argue that the idea of progressing toward rational cosmopolitanism is regulative, enabling us to look at the world *as if* humanity were on a just historical trajectory, then later liberal *and* poststructuralist thinkers gave ever more force to the ideal of futurity. There are claims that history is *actually* converging toward postideological recognition where we all realize that every other subject bears their own right to a world,[14] but claims for the *virtual* idea of a just future range from Derrida's "future-to-come" to Luce Irigaray's sense of "felicity in history" and Jürgen Habermas's "post-metaphysical" ideal of consensus.[15] In postapocalyptic cinema, a venal humanity appears to have ravaged the world, which has been laid to waste by overconsumption and self-interest, and yet it is *this* world that must be saved and *this* world that appears to save others, even if most of those poor-in-world others provide a violent backdrop for the heroic narrative. The resource-depleted United States that opens *Interstellar* or the world saved from nonbeing by the biotech corporations that control life in *Blade Runner 2049* are depictions of actual humanity's destructive past, even if those very scenes of depletion also demand future redemption. The corporate and capitalist powers that have reduced the world to nothing more than material for commodification are vanquished by a heroic and truly human fragment that has its eye on the families and children of the future (*Interstellar*) or the miracle of technology-free childbirth (*Blade Runner 2049*).

This species bifurcation that is so common in postapocalyptic cinema, for all its manifest dualism, occludes the constitutive apartheid of the Anthropocene. The world has, in fact, been divided between those who colonize, enslave, and consume the globe for the sake of a "technological maturity" and those humans who bear the burden of outsourced fragility. But it is not *this* difference that structures postapocalyptic culture. Rather than thinking of the ways in which destruction has been distributed and in which the stability and sustainability of the West has been secured by generating volatility and vulnerability elsewhere, postapocalyptic culture renders this geopolitical plane into a moral and cinematic question. Either by being confronted by impending disaster or suffering from a fall into mere survival, what is depicted as humanity sloughs off its less-than-human past and allows its properly human form to emerge. A self-enslaved humanity—shackled by its lesser tendencies—casts off what it has actually been, in order to emerge as the incarnation of its proper and always virtual potential.

The human is a being at war with itself, always at risk of failing to be what it properly is, always looking at its less-than-rational or enslaved self with a negating horror that marks its very essence. The figure of slavery, and especially slavery as Blackness, is deployed to set this internal battle between human and inhuman outside the body of white reason.[16] The use of slavery as an internal threat to who we are takes a political history of violence and produces an ontology; it ultimately makes sense to claim, as Frank Wilderson will do so insistently, that Black = African = nonhuman. In a quite concrete sense, humanity is possible because of the theft of labor and life of slavery:

> But African, or more precisely Blackness, refers to an individual who is by definition always already void of relationality. Thus modernity marks the emergence of a new ontology because it is an era in which an entire race appears, people who, a priori, that is prior to the contingency of the "transgressive act" (such as losing a war or being convicted of a crime), stand as socially dead in relation to the rest of the world. This, I will argue, is as true for those who were herded onto the slave ships as it is for those who had no knowledge whatsoever of the coffles. In this period, chattel slavery, as a condition of ontology and not just as an event of experience, stuck to the African like Velcro. To the extent that we can think the essence of Whiteness and the essence of Blackness, we must think their essences through the structure of the Master/Slave relation.[17]

This ontology of enslavement becomes increasingly apparent with European traditions of the Enlightenment and its aftermath; if one removes transcendent norms and can no longer justify worldly subjection by way of referring to slaves by nature or a divine right of kings, one has to explain how it is that this world is so unequal and unjust. How did priests and kings seize control of reason? If humans are not naturally fallen, how do we justify this world? The myth and figure of self-enslavement goes a long way. In *The Marriage of Heaven and Hell* William

Blake argued that our capacity to view the world as poets—seeing the world as animated with spirits—contracts when the priests take hold of the imagination; we become enslaved to our own tendency to view the world as so much dead matter at the mercy of calculation. Our manacles are "mind forg'd."[18] From early Romanticism to new forms of vital materialism, it seems that all we need to do is *see* the world with a life and spirit that connects us all; relationality is there if only we realize:

> Glove, pollen, rat, cap, stick. As I encountered these items, they shimmied back and forth between debris and thing-between, on the one hand, stuff to ignore, except insofar as it betokened human activity (the workman's efforts, the litterer's toss, the rat-poisoner's success), and, on the other hand, stuff that commanded attention in its own right, as existents in excess of their association with human meanings, habits, or projects. In the second moment, stuff exhibited its thing-power: it issued a call, even if I did not quite understand what it was saying. At the very least, it provoked affects in me: I was repelled by the dead (or was it merely sleeping?) rat and dismayed by the litter, but I also felt something else: a nameless awareness of the impossible singularity of that rat, that configuration of pollen, that otherwise utterly banal, mass-produced plastic water-bottle cap. . . .
>
> When the materiality of the glove, the rat, the pollen, the bottle cap, and the stick started to shimmer and spark, it was in part because of the contingent tableau that they formed with each other, with the street, with the weather that morning, with me. For had the sun not glinted on the black glove, I might not have seen the rat; had the rat not been there, I might not have noted the bottle cap, and so on. But they were all there just as they were, and so I caught a glimpse of an energetic vitality inside each of these things, things that

I generally conceived as inert. In this assemblage, objects appeared as things, that is, as vivid entities not entirely reducible to the contexts in which (human) subjects set them, never entirely exhausted by their semiotics.[19]

The relation between humans and things is a question of altering one's vision, of renewing one's relation to things *and their relationality*. Vibrant materialism, some modes of new materialism, and some modes of object-oriented ontology rely on this ongoing sense that the human as a separate subject is a myth that needs to be overcome by renewing and seeing into the life of things. What I have suggested in the preceding chapters is that this notion of saving our fallen vision by seeing into the life of things extends a long history of humanism that has warded off self-loss by way of renewed perception. There will always be a "new world" to save us from ourselves. In this maneuver, humanity seemingly restores itself to itself and gives life to a world that is no longer a mere thing. In actuality, this history has been a history of slavery and colonization, adopting a gaze toward *things that resist relationality* and that appear as both strangely other than human. As long as the figure and dialectic of the human is one of self-loss, self-enslavement, and self-redemption, the actual bifurcation of the world—the consignment of many humans to nonrelational yet wondrous things—will be occluded.

What happens when those others, who were once constitutive of the human in their negation, look upon this cinematic animal that calls itself humanity? There is a large body of work written from precisely this point of view or—more accurately—*many* points of view that look upon the human with the same puzzlement that anthropology directed toward those others of the worlds it deemed to be not quite human. As I have already suggested, the cinema of Jordan Peele can also be read as an allegory of white humanism, so that whiteness becomes the problem to be explained and not the ground of the world that needs to be redeemed. *Get Out* depicts an apparent reverence for Black culture that turns out to be a homegrown body-snatching business; the adoration of Black athleticism turns out to be the first stage in a brain-transplant scheme that allows whiteness to save itself by stealing the physicality and vision of Black bodies. *Us* depicts contemporary America as able to survive *only* if it continually tethers itself to a world of others whom it must also annihilate. *Nope* ties cinematic enjoyment and consumption to the animalization and annihilation of others. The destruction of these scenes of visual pleasure is both the end of the world and the possibility of freedom. What is made explicit in such affirmative imaginings of the end of the world is that saving *our world* requires the consumption and destruction of those whom the world has negated and that the "we" and the "us" that is presupposed by the attachment to the human is also bound up with no less powerfully affective exclusions.

While postapocalyptic Hollywood blockbuster cinema works by separating us from them, enabling a renewed humanity to save the world and the future, there is no shortage of work that focuses on the micro- and macroaggressions that form the unity of who we are. Claudia Rankine's *Just Us*, exploring a different sense of "us" from Peele's "us" of existentially annihilating America, opens the question of whether there might be a more deliberative "us," "we," or citizenship that does not involve the ongoing annihilation of Black life. Ostensibly, Rankine's project in *Just Us* remains within the conversation of who we are, opening with the questions of who is speaking and to whom *and* whether the affective exhaustion of reading and viewing so many images of who we are might generate a future. "How does one say / what if / without reproach?"[20]

Rankine's desired conversation that would converge toward

citizenship requires fragmentation. But there are two modes of fragmentation running through *Just Us*. The first is a fragmentation required by complexity, where the subject is belied by simple words of description. One must fragment syntax in order to be faithful to the intensity of damaged life:

> What if you are responsible to saving more than to
>   changing?
> What if you're the destruction coursing beneath
> your language of savior? Is that, too, not fucked up?
> You say, if other white people had not . . . or if it seemed like
> not enough . . . I would have . . .[21]

If fragmentation is what allows a subject to speak and pose the questions occluded by everyday speech and its comforts, the second fragmentation is destructive. Graphs, screenshots, images, and texts cut into the subject as if they were so many found objects. One might think of the first fragmentation as existential, such that poetry's destruction of textual coherence comes closer to the intensity and complexity of experience, while the second mode of fragmentation destroys the capacity to exist in this world. The nexus of these two modes of fragmentation is at its most intense in Rankine's poetic inscription of microaggression. On the one hand, *Just Us* seeks to forge a conversation; and yet at crucial moments, the poet's interlocutor seems to be unaware of the affective force or violence of their speech: "Was he thinking out loud? Were the words just slipping out before he could catch them? Was this the innocence of white privilege? Was he yanking my chain? Was he snapping the white-privilege flag in my face?"[22]

These questions both seek conversation and recognize its difficulty. The text—like Rankine's *Citizen: An American Lyric*—is interrupted with images that are, in part, evidence of the difficulties of being able to speak and, in part, interruptions.[23] There is something countercinematic and counterapocalyptic in this formal procedure—the drive toward coherence of voice and expression is broken apart by images that are *not* synthesized or rendered coherent. Just as the images break into the unity of voice, the text as a whole strives toward a conversation that is also a constant battle with the world. In *Just Us* the poet shows the price to be paid for "staying in the room"; one either hears and speaks to the violence of the conversation or remains silent, allowing the conversation to continue but *without* the forms of "we" or "us" that the volume seeks to bring into being or at least intimate. In *Just Us*, lines of poetry are cut into by racist tweets, screenshots, facsimiles of Jefferson's *Notes on the State of Virginia*, social science data, and demographics. An apparent opposition between a complex and fragmented poetry of the subject and a world of banal white privilege falls apart when Rankine's conversation itself becomes a form in which one chooses to stay in the room and keep the world going or hear and speak to what is happening and thereby end the conversation and end the world.

Rankine's ongoing attempt to find a "we" that would include her own citizenship is perhaps the least world-destructive way of thinking critically about the presupposed humanity of the world. Other modes, such as the various threads of Afropessimism that Rankine cites, are explicit and affirmative about ending the world and breaking free from the humanity defined through the negation of Blackness. Such resistant work is not simply oppositional but rather takes up the very problem of the opposition. What does it mean when an all-inclusive and presupposed "we" that takes itself to be the world and the human creates a narrative of salvation and inclusion that requires the nonbeing and disposability of so many others? This is what makes the image of Hands across America so powerful in *Us*; the homely unity of America is the end of the world. Taking up this point of view, the voice of what Fanon referred to as the "wretched" and what Afropessimism (after Fanon) has referred to as nonbeing, several theoretical approaches generate the destruction of the "we" that would take the form of what David Marriott (following Fanon) has referred to as invention. The "we" does not yet exist but comes to be through a destruction of the colonial relation: "The will of the people can only return to itself as self-present after a delay, or deferral; it can only perform itself as a people insofar as "the people" is exterior to, and comes to supplement, its own will. As soon as there is anything politically like the people's will, the people itself errs passively (since what defines it is just the suspended possibility of the sovereign constitution of itself as a people)."[24]

Marriott also argues, again following Fanon, that "racial slavery is not slavery as philosophically understood."[25] A politics focused on saving who *we* are relies on a ground that will fulfill itself, with any failure, impediment, or suffering resulting in the affective negation of *them*. To act as if there were no "we" renders political invention disturbingly and violently *impolitic*, and yet this is the only way in which the same dull round of saving who we are (with its ongoing violence) might be ruptured. One might mark a difference between philosophy's historical use of the slave motif, where from Plato to Nietzsche the human is this being who can always subject itself to a petrified image of itself, and racial slavery, where the already racialized unconscious is so at odds with the normativity of the human that it tears the human of reason apart from itself. As Marriott argues, with respect to decolonization and sovereignty, the absence of any "we" that could give a ground to revolutionary and world-ending violence cannot be an unfolding of the human but rather has to be a negation of the "petrification" that occupies consciousness: "The masses have to both perform and invent themselves in the event of indecision. The fact that this is what the wretched show should not be lost sight of; invention is the stage on which 'the people' can be both resuscitated and shattered, and precisely because it is not easy to be freed from the contagion of petrification."[26]

The *philosophical* motif of slavery plays itself out with increasing intensity in end-of-world culture; we are all at risk of becoming enslaved, becoming *like them*, because of *them*. Saving our world—saving humanity—appears as that which will save *them*, so much so that they do all they can to save us. The literature, cinema, and theory of racial slavery creates a different story; the end of the world, and the end of *us*, would unleash something other than the relational "we" of humanist recognition.

The end of the world yields two cinematic possibilities. The first, as I have indicated, is the cinematic comportment of humanity, where one views the present as divided between an unfortunate past of disintegration and a proper future of universal recognition. This humanity, or anthropos, and its capacity to take up an elevated command of history becomes increasingly entwined with forms of what Bostrom has referred to as "technological maturity," where one maximizes "intelligence" and liberates oneself from mere immediacy. On this account, humanity saves itself from its tendency toward slavery by imagining every other potential subject as similarly oriented toward an ideal of global humanity; deep down, ideally, everyone is like *us*, with our unique differences all contributing to our expansive sense of human expression. In postapocalyptic cinema, we constantly see this intimate relation between the parochial and the global; it is from the elevated point of human recognition— especially where the United States saves the world—that we all become one. Every individual already harbors a humanity that could be the ground of recognition for every other individual. In twenty-first-century Anthropocene discourse, humanity as some cerebral idea has been replaced by the tough reality of anthropos—where we are all united by occupying the same living system that is the earth, shifting the emphasis toward an utterly realist sense that we are all interconnected.

The second cinematic comportment forges a viewpoint that is inhuman, not so much cosmopolitan (imagining everyone as just like me) but cosmic—not a polity or connectedness that includes the globe but a sense that the globe, our world, is a fragment of a larger plane that it can barely grasp. Nietzsche opens his essay on truth and lies (with consciousness itself and its enslavement to truth as the greatest lie) from the viewpoint of an extraterrestrial observer: "Once upon a time, in some out of the way corner of that universe which is dispersed into numberless twinkling solar systems, there was a star upon which clever beasts invented knowing. That was the most arrogant and mendacious minute of 'world history,' but nevertheless, it was only a minute. After nature had drawn a few breaths, the star cooled and congealed, and the clever beasts had to die."[27] In the twentieth century, Deleuze would argue, following Nietzsche, that the history of cinema traces a path from techniques of montage, where images are cut and rearranged to indicate a broader harmonious whole, thereby capturing a complex movement no human eye could discern, toward cutting images from the human eye *and* this world. In part, Deleuze is reinforcing and intensifying a tradition that elevates thinking above day-to-day perception, suggesting that our proper future is one of liberation from mere immediacy; at the same time, Deleuze raises the question of whether this elevation is human and whether some grasp of the cosmos requires exiting the notion of history as the fulfilment of who we ought to be or properly are. What looks like a high philosophical tension in his work is played out with far less subtlety with every postapocalyptic disaster epic of our time. Let us imagine that humanity becomes most noble when it liberates itself from mere survival, has some higher grasp beyond its own time, and learns to live and think *for the future*. One might think of this, to use various philosophical terms, as transcendence, spirit, the virtual, or the idea. The problem, though, is when this supposedly transcendent or higher idea is *really* a fragment of the present that has elevated itself as the proper form of humanity in general. When postapocalyptic cinema depicts the end of Manhattan or the end of capitalism as the end of the world and does so through a heroic narrative of casting off the past for the sake of a redeemed future, we get a very clear sense of the constitutive border between humanism and its others. This is a cinema and posthumanism of *ressentiment*—we become who we ought to be by casting off who we have been in order to avoid becoming *them*.

One might contrast the virtual and ideal humanity of postapocalyptic cinema, where the actual history of violence reaches a fever pitch to reveal what humanity ought to have been all along, with an inhuman planetary eternity that grants force to what may have no bearing on our world. This contrast that I am drawing is easier said than done, for (at least) two reasons. First, the value we place today on the inhuman, posthuman, and cosmic dimensions is bound up with a long history that defines humanity as that unique being who can intuit what is beyond his own life. It is one of the features of the humanist tradition that however we define humanity, what is deemed to be valuable has some transcendent quality. We are those beings who can gaze into the cosmos with a sense of the infinite; we are those beings whose thinking and survival is oriented to a thoroughly open future. As I have already suggested, even before the advent of cinema, this comportment toward a sense of the open whole, where we look at the world as an ongoing expression of something like humankind or sense that reaches its fulfilment in global recognition, is crucial to Western humanism. It is not simply that one universalizes one's own sense of the human but rather that figures of the way in which one thinks about what is outside or beyond the self have a specific aesthetic form and comportment. It is one's capacity to see "eternity in a grain of sand," to quote William Blake.[28] What one might oppose to this would be to regard sand itself as composing an eternity that includes us and that does not require our intuition.

This brings me to the second problem with valorizing "the outside," or "unthought," as the privileged figure for saving the world. Everyday life may be mired in survival and existence; but when world-ending catastrophe strikes, humanity becomes what it ought to be, sacrificing immediacy for the sake of who we are. It is by way of panoramic elevation that a heroic fragment of humanity is capable of overcoming the wreckage of the past in order to save the world for us—we visionary beings. Just as elevating oneself above the human is typically the most human of gestures, so are various redemptive turns to the non-Western and *noncinematic* outside. Both *Mad Max: Fury Road* and *Avatar* ostensibly pit Western acquisitiveness and world-wasting violence against quasi-Indigenous forms of world attunement, but like many of their philosophical counterparts, the Indigenous outside not only serves to shore up the world in general (the West) but also is always a homely and assimilable outside. What cannot be admitted are the forms of non-Western thought that identify what we seek to save—the world—as precisely what must be ended. The cityscape that is so often the fully human center from which the globe is viewed, and that is the pocket of humanity that must survive as the rest of the planet falls into chaos, is a monument to cinematic humanity. It is only with the technological maturity and intensity of urban affluence that something like the human of the Anthropocene becomes possible. If *Avatar* and *Mad Max: Fury Road* gesture to non-Western forms of existence, they do so not to end this world but to find its better and world-saving other. One might argue, following Aileen Moreton-Robinson, that the images of urban space that typify the world are monuments to white possession and that cinematic dramas that flirt with the loss *and saving* of these urban spaces are collective exercises in reinforcing the human as a cinematic animal. What is unthinkable is that this built-up world of possession might give way to forms of sovereignty not marked by global survey:

> For Indigenous people, white possession is not unmarked, unnamed, or invisible; it is hypervisible. In our quotidian encounters, whether it is on the streets of Otago or Sydney, in the tourist shops in Vancouver or Waipahu, or sitting in a restaurant in New York, we experience ontologically the effects of white possession. These cities signify with every building and every street that this land is now possessed by others; signs of white possession are embedded everywhere in the landscape. The omnipresence of Indigenous sovereignties exists here too, but it is disavowed through the materiality of these significations, which are perceived as evidence of ownership by those who have taken possession. This is territory that has been marked by and through violence and race. Racism is thus inextricably tied to the theft and appropriation of Indigenous lands in the first world. In fact, its existence in the United States, Canada, Australia, Hawai'i, and New Zealand was dependent on this happening. The dehumanizing impulses of colonization are successfully acted upon because racisms in these countries are predicated on the logic of possession.[29]

By referring to the hypervisibility of white possession, Moreton-Robinson wants to *mark* the point of view from which the rest of the world, including Indigenous worlds, are normally surveyed. Rather than take the postapocalyptic, cinematic, and

Anthroposcenic point of view that surveys the globe in order to find a redemptive outside that will save its own world, she suggests that what is depicted as the world—the cityscape of civilization—needs to be viewed as that which must come to an end. The city, she argues, is—for those dispossessed—an ongoing monument to colonization. It is also the home of the point of view that will survey the world as an arena of cultural difference, where it is always empire's others who will carry the burden of difference and visibility.

Rather than seeing the prehistory of planetary destruction as a vote of no confidence, Anthropocene discourse has depicted the wake of wreckage as an imperative to be born anew. The present is increasingly *post*apocalyptic precisely by way of refusing to sweep away the world as it is now for a radically different future. Instead, all that can be imagined is the loss of the past. By depicting humanity as somehow overcome, fallen, or burdened with a tendency toward self-enslavement, it becomes possible, even necessary, to look to the future as the horizon that will allow a proper humanity to emerge. The cinematic conceit of a threatened world arriving at universal harmony is, in part, a continuation of Christian redemption narratives, where a fall from grace allows for a heightened sense of paradise regained, and, in part, an utterly secular insistence that the *only* paradise for humanity is *this* world in an ever so slightly adapted form. The past cannot be mere wreckage, and humanity cannot be what it has happened to be. This world must be a midway point between a past in which paradise was lost and a future when it will be regained, being all the greater for having been hidden for so long. It would not take much to take postapocalyptic and Anthropocene thought at its word—but as a first, and not last, word. If saving *the* world has always required saving an "us" from a "them" and if the end of the world has been depicted by using the landscapes and conditions that we have demanded of them, then the end of the world might be thought affirmatively as the end of *us*, the end of an absolute right to life and the beginning of the thought of what other lives might matter.

Ends

This book has been about cinema and the cinematic, but it has also been about theory, philosophy, and affect—everything that produces the sentiment and sense of the right we have to life. In many ways, the most profound text of philosophy that has confronted the end of the world as the end of *us* is Jordan Peele's *Us*, with its existential questioning of who we kill and consume to save the world and of who we are. In many ways, the most important cinematic text for thinking about the end of the world is not a film but an attempt at a conversation. Claudia Rankine's *Just Us* tries to compose a new "we" not dependent on the day-to-day violence of citizenship and ownness; the very lyric that would compose us is also fractured by the images that reflect and refract who we are. Hollywood cinema has been one of the most intense industries for manufacturing and saving the world, but it is not alone. Its affirmation of a humanity that is "too big to fail" is reiterated in government policy that will do all it can to shore up the world while doing very little to acknowledge the violence that composes the world. What has come to be known as the human, or anthropos, has been made *and* undone through cinema, literature, philosophy, and the affective sphere of twenty-first-century liberalism. Hollywood cinema sharpens the daily attachments that compose who we are, but that same industry has its rare but insistent moments of self-critique. The novel has a long history of promulgating possessive individualism, with its marriage plots, tales of fortune, and affirmations of the private spaces of acquisition and consumption, but the novel also has the space and capacity to question our attachment to who we are and the world we seek to save. Cinema, literature, philosophy, theory, art—all these ways in which worlds are formed and preserved are also events of damage and loss. What would you do, and who would you kill to save the world?

NOTES

I. IT'S NOT THE END OF THE WORLD

1. Dipesh Chakrabarty, "The Climate of History: Four Theses," *Critical Inquiry* 35, no. 2 (Winter 2009): 197–222.

2. Slavoj Žižek, *Pandemic! Covid-19 Shakes the World* (Cambridge: Polity, 2020).

3. Stephen Pinker, *The Better Angels of Our Nature: Why Violence Has Declined* (New York: Penguin, 2011).

4. Naomi Klein, *This Changes Everything: Capitalism vs. the Climate* (New York: Simon and Schuster, 2014).

5. Nicholas G. Carr, *The Shallows: What the Internet Is Doing to Our Brain* (New York: Norton, 2010); Adam Alter, *Irresistible: The Rise of Technology and the Business of Keeping Us Hooked* (New York: Penguin, 2017).

6. Gottfried Wilhelm Leibniz, *Theodicy: Essays on the Goodness of God, the Freedom of Man, and the Origin of Evil*, ed. Austin Farrar, trans. E. M. Huggard (Chicago: Open Court, 1998).

7. David Benatar, *Better Never to Have Been: The Harm of Coming into Existence* (Oxford: Clarendon Press, 2006).

8. Susan Neiman, *Evil in Modern Thought: An Alternative History of Philosophy* (Princeton NJ: Princeton University Press, 2002).

9. Immanuel Kant, "Idea for a Universal History with a Cosmopolitan Purpose," in *Kant: Political Writings*, ed. Hans Reiss, trans. H. B. Nisbet (Cambridge: Cambridge University Press, 1970), 41–53, 52.

10. Pinker, *Better Angels of Our Nature*; Francis Fukuyama, *The End of History and the Last Man* (New York: Free Press, 1992).

11. Luce Irigaray, *I Love to You: Sketch of a Possible Felicity in History*, trans. Alison Martin (London: Routledge, 2016).

12. Joseph Conrad, *Heart of Darkness*, ed. Ross C. Murfin (London: Palgrave 1996), 21.

13. Jean-Jacques Rousseau, *The Social Contract, and Other Later Political Writings*, ed. and trans. Victor Gourevitch (Cambridge: Cambridge University Press, 1997), 41.

14. William Blake, *Songs of Innocence and Experience: Shewing the Two Contrary States of the Human Soul, 1789–1794* (Oxford: Oxford University Press, 1970), 150.

15. Bernard Stiegler, *What Makes Life worth Living: On Pharmacology*, trans. Daniel Ross (Cambridge: Polity, 2013), 4.

16. Edmund Husserl, *The Crisis of the European Sciences and Transcendental Phenomenology*, trans. David Carr (Evanston: Northwestern University Press, 1970).

17. Martin Heidegger, "Letter on 'Humanism,'" in *Pathmarks*, ed. William McNeill (Cambridge: Cambridge University Press, 1998), 239–76.

18. Martin Heidegger, *Being and Time*, trans. Joan Stambaugh, rev. Dennis J. Schmidt (Albany: SUNY Press, 2010), 19; Ezra Pound, "Extract from 'A Retrospective,'" in *Literary Essays of Ezra Pound*, ed. T. S. Eliot (London: Faber, 1954), 3–8.

19. James Baldwin, "Everybody's Protest Novel," in *Notes of a Native Son* (Boston: Beacon Press, 1984), 13–23.

20. Fukuyama, *End of History*.

21. Nick Bostrom, "Existential Risk Prevention as Global Priority," *Global Policy* 4, no. 1 (2013): 15–31.

22. "Seeds of a Good Anthropocene," Future Earth, accessed October 18, 2018, https://futureearth.org/initiatives/other-initiatives/seeds -of-a-good-anthropocene/.

23. Clive Hamilton, *Earthmasters: The Dawn of the Age of Climate Engineering* (New Haven CT: Yale University Press, 2013), 207–8.

24. Lee Edelman, *No Future: Queer Theory and the Death Drive* (Durham NC: Duke University Press, 2004).

25. Rebekah Sheldon, *The Child to Come: Life after the Human Catastrophe* (Minneapolis: University of Minnesota Press, 2016), 36.

26. Chakrabarty, "Climate of History."

27. Martha C. Nussbaum, *Political Emotions: Why Love Matters for Justice* (Cambridge MA: Belknap Press, 2013).

28. Eric Schliesser, ed., *Sympathy: A History* (Oxford: Oxford University Press, 2015).

29. Gilles Deleuze, *The Fold: Leibniz and the Baroque*, trans. Tom Conley (Minneapolis: University of Minnesota Press, 1993), 19.

30. John Rawls, *A Theory of Justice* (Cambridge MA: Belknap Press, 1971).

31. Eduardo Viveiros de Castro, *Cannibal Metaphysics*, ed. and trans. Peter Skafish (Minneapolis: University of Minnesota Press, 2014), 55–56.

32. Thomas Nagel, "What Is It like to Be a Bat?," *The Philosophical Review* 83, no. 4 (1974), 435–50.

33. Stephen Jay Gould, "The Golden Rule—A Proper Scale for Our Environmental Crises," in *The Earth Around Us: Maintaining a Livable Planet*, ed. Jill S. Schneidermann (New York: W. H. Freeman, 2000), 112–19, 113–14.

34. Gould, "Golden Rule," 117.

35. Gould "Golden Rule," 119.

36. Christine M. Korsgaard, *Fellow Creatures: Our Obligations to Other Animals* (Oxford: Oxford University Press, 2018).

37. Christine M. Korsgaard, *Self-Constitution: Agency, Identity, and Integrity* (Oxford: Oxford University Press, 2009).

38. Friedrich Nietzsche, *On the Genealogy of Morality*, ed. Keith Ansell Pearson, trans. Carol Diethe (Cambridge: Cambridge University Press, 2006), 67.

39. Edmund Husserl, *Ideas: General Introduction to Pure Phenomenology, First Book*, trans. F. Kersten (Dordrecht, Netherlands: Kluwer, 1983).

40. This is what Heidegger referred to as "being-in-the-world," in *Being and Time*.

41. Quentin Meillassoux, *After Finitude: An Essay on the Necessity of Contingency*, trans. Ray Brassier (London: Continuum, 2008).

42. Jonathan Bennett, "Spinoza's Metaphysics," in *The Cambridge Companion to Spinoza*, ed. D. Garrett (Cambridge: Cambridge University Press, 1996).

43. Heidegger, *Being and Time*.

44. Martin Heidegger, *The Fundamental Concepts of Metaphysics: World, Finitude, Solitude*, trans. William McNeill and Nicholas Walker (Bloomington: Indiana University Press, 1995), 177.

2. TECHNOLOGIES OF THE SELF

1. Gilles Deleuze and Félix Guattari, "1837: Of the Refrain," in *A Thousand Plateaus: Capitalism and Schizophrenia*, trans. Brian Massumi (Minneapolis: University of Minnesota Press, 1987), 310–50.

2. Peter Brooks, *Reading for the Plot: Design and Intention in Narrative* (Cambridge MA: Harvard University Press, 1984).

3. Alasdair MacIntyre, *After Virtue: A Study in Moral Theory*, 3rd ed. (Notre Dame IN: University of Notre Dame Press, 2007), 31–32.

4. Macintyre, *After Virtue*, 240.

5. Macintyre, *After Virtue*, 25.

6. Laura Marcus, "Modernist Literature and Film," in *Bloomsbury Companion to Modernist Literature*, ed. Ulrika Maude and Mark Nixon (London: Bloomsbury, 2018), 153–70.

7. Bret Easton Ellis, *American Psycho* (New York: Vintage 1991).

8. Bernard Stiegler, *Technic and Time*, vol. 3, *Cinematic Time and the Question of Malaise*, trans. Stephen Barker (Stanford: Stanford University Press, 2011).

9. Peter Szendy, *Apocalypse Cinema: 2012 and Other Ends of the World* (New York: Fordham University Press, 2015).

10. Bernard Stiegler, "The Proletarianization of Sensibility," trans. Arne De Boever, *boundary 2* 44, no. 1 (2017): 5–18.

11. Bernard Stiegler, *Decadence of Industrial Democracies*, trans. Daniel Ross (Cambridge, UK: Polity 2011) 26–27, emphasis in the original.

12. Aimé Césaire, *The Complete Poetry of Aimé Césaire*, bilingual ed., trans. A. James Arnold and Clayton Eshleman (Middletown CT: Wesleyan University Press, 2017). See also John E. Drabinski, "Césaire's Apocalyptic Word," *South Atlantic Quarterly* 115, no. 3 (2016): 567–84.

13. Deleuze and Guattari, *A Thousand Plateaus*, 232–309.

14. Immanuel Kant, *Critique of Pure Reason*, ed. and trans. Paul Guyer and Allen Wood (Cambridge: Cambridge University Press, 1998), A100–101, 229.

15. Henri Bergson, *Creative Evolution*, trans. Arthur Mitchell (New York: Modern Library, 1911, 1944), 332.

16. Gilles Deleuze, *Cinema 2: The Time-Image*, trans. Hugh Tomlinson and Robert Galeta (Minneapolis: University of Minnesota Press, 1989).

3. SAVE THE WORLD

1. Future Earth, accessed October 24, 2022, https://futureearth.org.

2. Earth Futures at UC Santa Cruz and UC Riverside, accessed October 24, 2022, https://earthfutures.sites.ucsc.edu.

3. Dominique Lestel, Jeffrey Bussolini, and Matthew Chrulew, "The Phenomenology of Animal Life," *Environmental Humanities* 5, no. 1 (2014): 125–48.

4. Bruce Pascoe, *Dark Emu: Aboriginal Australia and the Birth of Agriculture* (London: Scribe, 2018); Roxanne Dunbar-Ortiz, *An Indigenous Peoples' History of the United States* (Boston: Beacon Press, 2014).

5. Richard David, "Farmers or Hunter-Gatherers? The Dark Emu Debate." *Arena Quarterly* 7 (September 2021), https://arena.org.au/dark-emus-critics/.

6. James C. Scott, *Against the Grain: A Deep History of the Earliest States* (New Haven CT: Yale University Press, 2017).

7. Emily St. John Mantel, *Station Eleven* (New York: Alfred A. Knopf, 2014).

8. Tim Mulgan, *Ethics for a Broken World: Imagining Philosophy after Catastrophe* (London: Acumen 2011).

9. Jean-Jacques Rousseau, "Discourse on the Origin of Inequality," in *Basic Political Writings of Jean Jacques Rousseau*, trans. Donald A. Cress (Indianapolis: Hackett, 1987), 25–82, 41.

10. Immanuel Kant, *Critique of the Power of Judgment*, ed. Paul Guyer, trans. Paul Guyer and Eric Matthews (Cambridge: Cambridge University Press, 2000), 5.427.

11. "Our Work," Future Earth, accessed October 24, 2022, https://futureearth.org/about/our-work/.

12. Stiegler, "The Proletarianization of Sensibility."

13. Bernard Stiegler, *The Neganthropocene*, ed. and trans. Daniel Ross (London: Open Humanities Press, 2018).

14. Nick Bostrom, "Existential Risk Prevention as Global Priority," *Global Policy* 4, no. 1 (2013): 15.

15. Bostrom, "Existential Risk Prevention as Global Priority," 15.

16. Bostrom, "Existential Risk Prevention as Global Priority," 18.

17. Eduardo Viveiros de Castro and Yuk Hui, "For a Strategic Primitivism: A Dialogue between Eduardo Viveiros de Castro and Yuk Hui," *Philosophy Today* 65, no. 2 (2021), 391–400.

18. Bostrom, "Existential Risk as Global Priority," 19.

19. Bostrom, "Existential Risk as Global Priority," 17.

20. Fredric Jameson, *The Seeds of Time* (New York: Columbia University Press, 1994).

21. Michel Foucault, *The Order of Things* (London: Tavistock, 1970).

22. Bruce D. Smith and Melinda A. Zeder, "The Onset of the Anthropocene," *Anthropocene* 4 (2013): 8–13.

23. Donna J. Haraway, *Staying with the Trouble: Making Kin in the Chthulucene* (Durham NC: Duke University Press, 2016); Jason Moore, ed., *Anthropocene or Capitalocene? Nature, History, and the Crisis of Capitalism* (Oakland: PM Press, 2016); Nicholas Mirzoeff, "It's Not the Anthropocene, It's the White Supremacy Scene; or, The Geological Color Line," in *After Extinction*, ed. Richard Grusin (Minneapolis: University of Minnesota Press), 123–50.

24. Lewis R. Gordon, "Race, Theodicy, and the Normative Emancipatory Challenges of Blackness," *South Atlantic Quarterly* 112, no. 4 (2013): 725–36.

25. Chakrabarty, "Climate of History."

26. Roland Barthes, *Mythologies*, trans. Annette Lavers (New York: Noonday Press, 1972), 128.

27. Theodor W. Adorno, *Aesthetic Theory*, ed. Gretel Adorno and Rolf Tiedemann, trans. Robert Hullot-Kentnor (London: Bloomsbury, 2013).

28. Bernard Stiegler, "Organology of Dreams and Archi-Cinema," *Nordic Journal of Aesthetics* 47 (2014): 7–37.

29. Yuk Hui, "Writing and Cosmotechnics," *Derrida Today* 13, no. 1 (2020): 17–32.

30. T. J. Demos, *Against the Anthropocene: Visual Culture and Environment Today* (Cambridge MA: MIT Press, 2017).

31. Kimon Lycos, *Plato on Justice and Power: Reading Book 1 of Plato's "Republic"* (Albany: State University of New York Press, 1987).

32. Bernard Stiegler, "The Quarrel of the Amateurs," *boundary 2* 44, no. 1 (2017): 35–52.

33. Kant, *Critique of the Power of Judgment*, 5.172.

34. Friedrich Nietzsche, *The Birth of Tragedy and Other Writings*, ed. Raymond Geuss and Ronald Speirs (Cambridge: Cambridge University Press, 1999).

35. Fredric Jameson, "Imaginary and Symbolic in Lacan: Marxism, Psychoanalytic Criticism, and the Problem of the Subject," *Yale French Studies* 55–56 (1977): 338–95.

36. Naomi Klein, *The Shock Doctrine: The Rise of Disaster Capitalism* (New York: Picador, 2007).

37. Carole Pateman, *The Sexual Contract* (Stanford: Stanford University Press, 1988).

38. Gilles Deleuze and Felix Guattari, *Anti-Oedipus: Capitalism and Schizophrenia*, trans. Robert Hurley, Mark Seem, and Helen R. Lane (Minneapolis: University of Minnesota Press 1983), 105.

39. Sigmund Freud, "Femininity," trans. James Strachey, lecture 23 in *New Introductory Lectures on Psychoanalysis, and Other Works*, vol. 22 of *The Standard Edition of the Complete Psychological Works of Sigmund Freud* (London: Hogarth Press, 1932–36).

40. Conrad, *Heart of Darkness*, 77.

41. David Marriott, *On Black Men* (Edinburgh: Edinburgh University Press, 2000); Tommy J. Curry, *The Man-Not: Race, Class, Genre, and the Dilemmas of Black Manhood* (Philadelphia PA: Temple University Press, 2017); Hortense J. Spillers, "Mama's Baby, Papa's Maybe: An American Grammar Book," *Diacritics* 17, no. 2 (1987): 64–81; C. Riley Snorton, *Black on Both Sides: A Racial History of Trans Identity* (Minneapolis: University of Minnesota Press, 2017).

42. "He had kicked himself loose of the earth. Confound the man! he had kicked the very earth to pieces." Conrad, *Heart of Darkness*, 83.

43. Paul de Man, "The Rhetoric of Temporality," in *Blindness and Insight: Essays in the Rhetoric of Contemporary Criticism* (Minneapolis: University of Minnesota Press, 1983), 187–228.

44. R. A. Judy, *Sentient Flesh: Thinking in Disorder, Poiesis in Black* (Durham NC: Duke University Press, 2020).

45. Orlando Patterson, *Slavery and Social Death: A Comparative Study*, with a new preface (Cambridge MA : Harvard University Press, 2018).

46. Stiegler, "Proletarianization of Sensibility."

47. Bernard Stiegler, *Technics and Time*, vol. 2, *Disorientation*, trans. Stephen Barker (Stanford: Stanford University Press, 2009).

48. Plato, *Republic*, trans. Paul Shorey, in *The Collected Dialogues of Plato, including the Letters*, ed. Edith Hamilton and Huntington Cairns (Princeton NJ: Princeton University Press, 1961), bk. 7, 514a–515b, 747.

49. Sylvia Wynter, *Sylvia Wynter: On Being Human as Praxis*, ed. Katherine McKittrick (Durham NC: Duke University Press, 2015), 21.

50. Will Steffen et al., "The Anthropocene: From Global Change to Planetary Stewardship," *Ambio* 40, no. 7 (November 2011): 739–61, https://www.ncbi.nlm.nih.gov/pmc/articles/PMC3357752/?tool =pmcentrez&report=abstract.

51. Kant, *Critique of the Power of Judgment*, 5.364.

52. Jacques Derrida, *Edmund Husserl's Origin of Geometry: An Introduction*, trans. John P. Leavey Jr. (Lincoln: University of Nebraska Press, 1989), 130.

53. Derrida, *Edmund Husserl's Origin of Geometry*, 81.

54. Jacques Derrida, "The Ends of Man," *Philosophy and Phenomenological Research* 30, no. 1 (1969): 31–57. On suspension, see Anne C. McCarthy, *Awful Parenthesis: Suspension and the Sublime in Romantic and Victorian Poetry* (Toronto: University of Toronto Press, 2018).

55. Wynter, *On Being Human as Praxis*, 24.

56. Hee-Jung S. Joo, "We Are the World (but Only at the End of the World): Race, Disaster, and the Anthropocene," *EPD* 38, no. 1 (2020): 72–90, 77–78.

57. Paul de Man, *Aesthetic Ideology*, ed. Andrzej Warminski (Minneapolis: University of Minnesota Press, 1996) 82.

58. Jean-Paul Sartre, *The Transcendence of the Ego: An Existentialist Theory of Consciousness*, trans. Forrest Williams and Robert Kirkpatrick (New York: Hill and Wang, 1960).

59. "I came into the world imbued with the will to find a meaning in things, my spirit filled with the desire to attain to the source of the world, and then I found that I was an object in the midst of other

objects." Frantz Fanon *Black Skin, White Masks*, trans. Charles Lam Markmann (London: Pluto Press, 1967), 109.

60. Geoffrey H. Hartman, "Romanticism and Anti-Self-Consciousness," *Centennial Review* 6, no. 4 (1962): 553–65.

61. Bernard Stiegler, *Technics and Time*, vol. 1, *The Fault of Epimetheus*, trans. Richard Beardsworth and George Collins (Stanford: Stanford University Press, 1998).

62. Wynter, *On Being Humans as Praxis*, 25.

63. Jane Bennett, *Vibrant Matter: A Political Ecology of Things* (Durham NC: Duke University Press, 2009).

64. Calvin Warren, *Ontological Terror: Blackness, Nihilism, and Emancipation* (Durham NC: Duke University Press, 2018).

65. Nick Bostrom, "In Defence of Posthuman Dignity," *Bioethics* 19, no. 3 (2005): 202–14.

66. Rosi Braidotti, *The Posthuman* (Cambridge, UK: Polity, 2013), 80.

67. Alexander G. Weheliye, *Habeas Viscus: Racializing Assemblages, Biopolitics, and Black Feminist Theories of the Human* (Durham NC: Duke University Press, 2014).

4. BIFURCATION

1. Sigmund Freud, "Civilization and Its Discontents," in *The Standard Edition of the Complete Psychological Works of Sigmund Freud*, vol. 21, *1927–1931: The Future of an Illusion, Civilization and its Discontents, and Other Works*, trans. James Strachey (London: Hogarth Press, 1961), 57–146.

2. Mark Larrimore, "Sublime Waste: Kant on the Destiny of the 'Races,'" in "Civilization and Oppression," supplementary issue, *Canadian Journal of Philosophy Supplementary* 25 (1999): 99–125.

3. "For all intents and purposes, the politics of melanin, not isolated in its strange powers from the imperatives of a mercantile and competitive economics of European nation-states, will make of 'transcendence' and 'degradation' the basis of a historic violence that will rewrite the histories of modern Europe and black Africa. These mutually exclusive nominative elements come to rest on the same governing semantics—the ahistorical, or symptoms of the 'sacred.'" Spillers, "Mama's Baby, Papa's Maybe," 71.

4. Haraway, *Staying with the Trouble*.

5. McKenzie Wark, "Make Kith Not Kin! On Donna Haraway," *Public Seminar*, June 24, 2016, https://publicseminar.org/2016/06/kith/.

6. Chakrabarty, "Climate of History."

7. Ray Kurzweil, *The Singularity Is Near: When Humans Transcend Biology* (New York: Penguin, 2005).

8. N. K. Jemisin, *The Fifth Season* (New York: Hachette, 2015).

9. Kandice Chuh, *The Difference Aesthetics Makes* (Durham NC: Duke University Press, 2019).

10. Mary Hesse, "Habermas' Consensus Theory of Truth," *PSA: Proceedings of the Biennial Meeting of the Philosophy of Science Association* 2 (1978): 373–96.

11. Kant, *Critique of the Power of Judgment* 20.224.

12. Lindsay Waters, "To Become What One Is: Why I Seek the Revival of Criticism," *boundary 2* 48, no. 1 (2021): 251–63.

13. Kim Stanley Robinson, *Ministry for the Future* (London: Orbit Books, 2020); Fredric Jameson, *The Political Unconscious: Narrative as a Socially Symbolic Act* (London: Methuen, 1981), 9.

14. Fukuyama, *End of History*; Pinker, *Better Angels of Our Nature*.

15. David Wood, "On Being Haunted by the Future," *Research in Phenomenology* 36 (2006): 274–298; Jürgen Habermas *Postmetaphysical Thinking II*, trans. Ciaran Cronin (Cambridge, UK: Polity, 2017).

16. Frank B. Wilderson III, *Afropessimism* (New York: Liveright, 2020).

17. Frank B. Wilderson III, *Red, White, and Black: Cinema and the Structure of U.S. Antagonisms* (Durham NC: Duke University Press, 2010), 18.

18. William Blake, "Auguries of Innocence," in *The Marriage of Heaven and Hell*, plate 11, in *The Complete Poetry and Prose of William Blake*, ed. David Erdman (New York: Anchor, 1988), 490.

19. Jane Bennett, *Vibrant Matter: A Political Ecology of Things* (Durham NC: Duke University Press, 2009), 4–5.

20. Claudia Rankine, "What If," in *Just Us: An American Conversation* (Minneapolis MN: Graywolf Press, 2020), stanza 1.

21. Rankine, "What If," stanza 4.

22. Claudia Rankine, "Liminal Spaces," in *Just Us*.

23. Claudia Rankine, *Citizen: An American Lyric* (Minneapolis MN: Graywolf Press, 2014).

24. David Marriott, *Whither Fanon? Studies in the Blackness of Being* (Stanford: Stanford University Press, 2018), 253.